D1713271

Bijou and the Trapdoor in the Floor

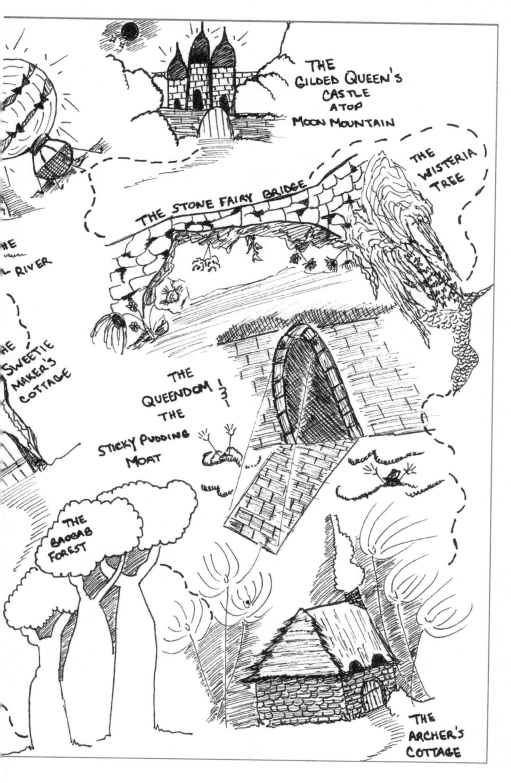

EX LIBRIS

Rowden Abbey, Herefordshire, UK.

# BIJOU
## AND THE
# TRAPDOOR
## IN THE
# FLOOR

A Tall Tale of the Wood

by
## E. J. ROWDON

Illustrations by
## NICOLA LECCIONES
&
## E. J. ROWDON

Archway Publishing books may be ordered through booksellers or by contacting:

Archway Publishing
1663 Liberty Drive
Bloomington, IN 47403
www.archwaypublishing.com

Because of the dynamic nature of the Internet, any web addresses or
links contained in this book may have changed since publication and
may no longer be valid. The views expressed in this work are solely those
of the author and do not necessarily reflect the views of the publisher,
and the publisher hereby disclaims any responsibility for them.

ISBN: 978-1-4808-4943-3 (hc)
ISBN: 978-1-4808-4942-6 (e)

Library of Congress Control Number: 2017919011

Print information available on the last page.

Archway Publishing rev. date: 12/12/2017

For Phoe, from me, this tall tale of the Wood

# Contents

Beware these curious characters and creatures ...


The Laughing Kookaburra—a *very* rude bird

The Pygmy—a mussssssic maker

The Great Auk—a prompt potter

The Sweetie Maker—a portly pie baker

Madam Loulou de la Mer—a gypsy fortune-teller

The Phoenix—a winged monster

The Giant Moa—a wanderer

The Archer—a madman

The Gilded Henchmen—the Queen's army

The Violet Fairy—a surly sprite

The Tree Spirits—the daydream nymphs

The Black Beast—the wretch's pest

The Gilded Queen of Moon Mountain—the wretch

The Tree Dweller—an enchanted drummer boy

*These*, you may trust, but all those not listed here or there, you should neither beware nor trust entirely...

Chirps—a sweet 'keet

Flora Bell—a curious cat

and ...

Bijou—a *very* curious child

# Prologue

When curious children creep beneath
The trapdoor in the floor,
They find the entrance to a wood—
One they'd never discovered before.
Legend tells that there a star will fall,
Brought with it a single wish.
And the beat of the Tree Dweller's drum
Shall lead the curious children to it.

# Chapter I

## The Trapdoor in the Floor

Every so often the most curious of children discover the Wood. They must go down to get up and through to get back, but they all find their way eventually.

*Bom-bom, bom-bom!* came a drum suddenly.

Bijou had never heard such a ruckus in all her young years—at least, not one that came from her very own dollhouse. After all, no one was home. She had just sent her paper dolls on a trip up the treacherous Moon Mountain, past the fearsome Black Beast, and to the Gilded Queen's castle. In other words, over the mossy hills in her backyard, past the family's sleeping Newfoundland, and to her mother's gardening shed. This is where her very stern mother kept her favorite golden-colored tolly briar seeds inside their worn gilded tin. Bijou was forbidden to meddle with them, for when her mother's prized tolly briars were in full bloom, their golden buds were the envy of every other mother on the lane, and how she *loved* to be envied.

*Bom-bom, bom-bom!* came the drum once more, and louder than before.

"They couldn't *possibly* be back from their journey yet, Chirps," Bijou remarked to her small yellow-and-white parakeet as it sat in its round gilded cage.

Bijou hopped off her gray-and-white rocking horse and knelt down to peek through the miniature windows of her Tudor-style dollhouse. Much like her own home, her paper dolls lived in a house made of crisscrossing timber beams, which could be seen from the exterior as well as from inside. The outer walls were covered with a lush green ivy that Bijou had snipped from the exterior of her own home and had strung about the tiny blue shutters. Like tidy book-ends, twin stone chimneys sat on either side of the house, and a black roof cupped the tops and sides of three small upper-story windows. To one side of the home was a red waterwheel, which when spun about churned a small blue pond. It was really just an old, cracked dish filled with tap water, but Bijou loved it best. She had even surrounded her pond with a garden of light-blue cotton poppies and blush-pink silk peonies that she'd crafted herself from her mother's quilting remnants. The dollhouse was quite to Bijou's liking, even if her stern mother thought it a waste of space in such an already cramped nursery.

There was no immediate evidence that Bijou's paper dolls had returned home from their trip. She saw no luggage being unpacked despite having just cut out a bright new wardrobe, and she could hear none of the homeowner's usual chatter. You see, the homeowners were the Papier family, whose dollhouse sat at Number Nine Nursery Row, and they were *always* chatting and causing a commotion. Bijou poked open the blue arched front door of the dollhouse with her finger to see if they'd left miniature muddy footprints from their travels, but there were no footprints and no one home.

*Bom-bom, bom-bom!* The mysterious drum sounded again, and determined, Bijou stood up and divided her dollhouse into its two large sections. She expected there would be nothing more beneath it than a worn section of wooden floorboards, but as she pushed the dollhouse open, it instead revealed a gilded trapdoor in the floor.

"*Goodness!* That *certainly* wasn't there before!" she exclaimed, inching backward to examine the trap.

Bijou knelt down again and tugged on a large gold-gilded knocker at the center of the trap and heaved the heavy wooden door open and upward. Her black cat scrambled suddenly from beneath the bed to peer and paw into the hole.

"*Oh*, you think so, Flora Bell?" Bijou remarked, making space next to him and straddling the sides of the trap.

She poked her head into the hole, expecting to find a dusty crawl space filled with families of mice and other rodents her mother had many times chased from their yard and gardening shed, but instead Bijou and Flora Bell could see their yard itself. The pair rushed to peer out of the nursery window and down into their yard, but it was still there, and everything in it was as it should be. They returned to the trapdoor, and Bijou attempted to keep her balance while digging her soft black buckled slippers into its frame.

"How did our garden get down *there*, Flora Bell?"

Flora Bell shook his head in bewilderment, for admittedly, he didn't know.

An unfamiliar, dark wood bordered the yard below, and a swift breeze began to blow from it and through Bijou's messy mane of yellow curls. Being a naturally curious child, she instantly had the sense to venture into the strange forest beneath the floor, but she knew her stern mother would insist that a girl of such considerable imagination would become something of a nuisance if left in a wood on her own. Or worse, dirtying her favorite scarlet dress and tearing yet another ruffled sleeve. Still, Bijou had tired of her paper dolls and, after all, had been down the hill and to the boundary of her yard many times and had never seen such a thick and dark forest.

*Bom-bom, bom-bom!* came the drum again just before a gilded butterfly fluttered beneath Bijou and began to tickle her nose with its delicate wings before disappearing into the Wood.

"Did you see *that*, Flora Bell?" she asked excitedly.

Flora Bell merely shook his head side to side, pretending that he hadn't.

"Chirps, do you suppose I should follow it?"

The nervous bird began to hop about in his cage, chirping a strong warning back at Bijou, but she ignored it, as she typically ignored most warnings.

She began eagerly lowering herself through the trapdoor, dangling for a moment, her small fingers clenching the frame.

"Darlings, I *promise* I'll be back. I've just got to see where that drum is coming from!" Bijou peered over her shoulder and attempted to build herself up enough to jump when she lost her grip suddenly and fell to the mossy ground below. She landed with a *thud* and could hear desperate meows and chirps coming from her nursery above, but as she glanced up at the trapdoor, it slammed shut and was far out of reach.

The beat of the drum from within the Wood began to quicken, and Bijou followed it, darting through the familiar garden, past the light-blue poppies and blush-pink peonies, and burst into the forest, ducking beneath low branches and leaping over downed logs. The once steady beat had begun to lessen and fade, and there were no other noises in the Wood, as if the forest had fallen asleep. This gave the curious child the distinct sense that the drum was running from her, and so she decided, despite her stern mother and panicked pets, that she would chase it.

# Chapter II

# The Kookaburra's Pond and the Gilded Windmill

Bijou could suddenly hear the scurrying of small creatures and rustling of bushes and leaves, as the trees and their inhabitants had now awakened. She rested in a clearing for a moment, realizing the scurrying and rustling stopped whenever she stopped, and she could feel the eyes of the forest upon her. Bijou would have never normally ventured into such a dark wood alone, but the resonating beat of the drum had pulsed down through her fingertips, and had made her brave, or at least braver than before.

The only discernible passage through the thick banyan trees was a narrow pathway that led to a giant moss-covered tree stump. The ancient banyan stump stood at least a story high and had a low archway cut into its middle.

"*Peculiar,*" Bijou remarked to herself as she passed through the archway and into the narrowing burrow.

The forest groaned behind her, and as she turned to run back

through the entrance to the hollowed stump, the thicket and brush began to grow and tangle quickly, creating a woven barrier between where she'd been already and where she would go.

"Oh *no!*" Bijou bellowed, pulling and kicking at the wall of thicket for a moment before tiring.

She dusted off her scarlet dress and primped the white ruffled slip that was peeking out from beneath its hem. Her very stern mother was always on her about keeping her clothes tidy, and thus, primping was something that Bijou did often when nervous.

"My advice to you," she began to herself, "is to avoid tearing or dirtying your clothes, as Mother will *already* be furious to learn that you've been lost in a wood. That is, if you should become *unlost,*" she trailed off nervously.

Bijou looked about timidly and then upward to the ceiling.

The tightly woven vines and pale purple flowers of a giant jacaranda tree had created a canopy above her, and the narrowing walls of the burrow were golden from top to bottom and lined with wooden carvings of curious characters and creatures, whose eyes followed Bijou as she walked. One of them, an archer, kneeling with his bow and arrow aimed high. Another, an oversized bird walking with a sack slung over his back. And yet another carving was of a large flying creature that looked more like a winged monster than a bird.

Even more curious were the floating white candles that lit the burrow and lined the passageway. On the ground beneath them were piles of clay pots marked *Jam & Jungle Jelly* and scattered glass apothecary bottles atop hovering golden shelves that read *Enchanted Tears* and *Baobab's Bark*.

"Such oddly labeled concoctions!" Bijou whispered excitedly, grazing the cork tops with her fingertips and tucking one that was labeled *Elephant's Wisdom* into her dress pocket. "You can never have too much wisdom or quite enough care," she recited, recalling her mother's constant advice, however seldom minded. It didn't seem to bother Bijou that the candles were floating on their own or the burrow had suddenly grown up all around her; she simply kept on, entranced with each little, odd item.

Bijou came quickly upon a second archway, and without noticing, the canopy and forest suddenly grew down the golden walls, taking back the burrow and sealing the passageway behind her. She ducked beneath the archway, stepping out into a vast sugarcane field of green stalks that stretched nine feet into the air and towered over her as they swayed back and forth on a breeze.

A narrow blue pond split the field down the middle and had giant metallic-blue lotus flowers clinging to one another and their sprawling greenery. Bijou pushed her way through the tight rows of sugarcane and toward the pond, brushing her fingers over the velvety petals of a drooping lotus as she arrived.

"Just one of these sparkling flowers would make a beautiful magic carpet for the Papier family! Yes, this one looks the right size, I think." But as Bijou bent over to pick the flower, a bird wearing a bright-blue bow tie around its thick neck came diving down through the air and pecked her on her hand.

"Ouch!" she cried, wrenching her hand back and petting it.

"Consider how the *lotus* would feel!" squawked the strange bird, perching atop a moss-covered log that lay along the edge of the pond. "They're falling asleep, you know. They'll be underwater by sundown!"

"I was merely picking a flower! You needn't peck me for *that*, bird!" Bijou snapped, still rubbing her wounded hand.

"*Kookaburra* is my name!" the bird insisted, ruffling his bands of blue and white feathers and puffing up his short but plump body. "*Laughing* Kookaburra of the Wood, to be precise!"

Bijou took a seat at the other end of the log. "*Laughing* Kookaburra? *Can* you laugh?"

"I'd say your feathers *are* frightful enough to laugh *at*," the Kookaburra snorted, breaking into a maniacal laugh that to Bijou sounded more like a monkey laughing than a bird call.

"*That* is a *very* rude remark!" Bijou scolded the bird, wagging her finger at him.

"It was just a joke, birdie. Don't you know any jokes?"

Bijou's frown eased slightly as she thought. "*Well*, my father taught me a rather good one, but I never can get it just right."

"What's his *name*?"

"*Father's* name?" Bijou thought for a moment. "I believe he's called William Sweet." She had to think on it. After all, Bijou never called her father by his true name.

"Don't you *know* what you call him?"

"But I *don't* call him by his *true* name. *Oh*, Mother wouldn't like that at all," she insisted.

"There are simply too many of us *not* to call a bird by his or her true name," remarked the Kookaburra.

"But what if two birds have the same name?" asked Bijou.

"Such a thing would be utter chaos!" squawked the bird. "Besides, there are plenty of names for everyone to have their own."

Bijou squinted both eyes and wrinkled her lips in disbelief. "You're the only *Laughing Kookaburra*?"

"Of *course*!" scoffed the bird. "My brothers are Snorting and Sobbing, and my wee sister is Shrieking."

*And his mother and father are Cooing and Cawing*, Bijou thought to herself, giggling.

"Now let me see," she began. "It *was* a rather funny joke that Father had taught me. It was something about a horse, or perhaps a cow. Well, anyway, I believe they were in a pasture one morning, and—"

"No bother!" the Kookaburra interrupted, hopping into the air repeatedly. "I know *plenty* of jokes!" He hopped quickly down the log toward Bijou and perched upon her knee. "For instance, if you please, *why* does a hummingbird hum?"

Bijou knew the sensible answer. "Well, they flap their wings so quickly that—"

"Tut-tut!" interrupted the bird. "It *hums* because it doesn't know the *words!*" The Kookaburra broke into hysterical laughter, rocking back and forth on his thin legs.

Bijou wrinkled her lips. The joke wasn't very funny, but she gave a slight giggle anyway, for fear he might think her rude. She rubbed his blue bow tie between her fingers, admiring the soft material.

"Such *lovely* silk," Bijou complimented as the bird hopped up her dress and into the palms of her hands. "I've never known a bird to wear clothes. I wonder if Chirps would like it if I started dressing him up."

"*Who* is *Chirps?*" scoffed the Kookaburra, puffing up his plump body once more. But before Bijou could reply, the flighty bird had already become disinterested. "Would you care to hear another joke?" he blurted. "*What* is smarter than a talking bird? Don't know? A *spelling bee!*" The Kookaburra began to laugh maniacally again, flying into the air then diving back down and landing on the log.

"You didn't give me enough time to guess," Bijou pouted, crossing her arms over her chest.

"A nit without wit is quick to *outwit*, throws a fit, then quickly quits," recited the bird, mocking her. "*You're* a nittiwathunger!"

Bijou's face turned blood-red. "I'm *not* a nit, nitty, nitta—well, whatever it is!" she stammered, jumping up from the log and dusting off her scarlet dress. "All *you* know are bird jokes! And anyway, they aren't very good."

The bird continued as if he hadn't heard her remark. "What did the chess piece say to the other before bedtime? Can't guess? Give up?

*Knight, knight!*" The Kookaburra lurched back and forth in laughter, and though once again she hadn't been given the chance to answer, Bijou couldn't help but to admit it *was* a clever joke.

"Well, I should be going," she said, waving at the obnoxious bird and turning to leave.

"Why, birdie, *why?*"

"Because I don't know where I am."

"You are in the Wood, birdie; now you know."

"*Yes*," she sighed. "Could you tell me how to get *out* of the Wood?"

"Why would you want to leave? It's nice here, don't you think?" The Kookaburra lifted into the air and dove down again to skim the surface of the water with his beak. Scooping up a drink, he flew back to Bijou and offered it to her.

"*Oh*, it's a lovely pond," she began, grimacing slightly and waving off the drink inside the bird's beak, "but I must get home. Mother and Father will be worried when they find out I'm not in the nursery."

"Is a nursery like a nest?" asked the Kookaburra.

"I suppose it *is*," said Bijou.

"*I* left the nest *ages* ago! Why, *you're* the biggest baby bird I've ever seen!" mocked the Kookaburra.

"*That* does it!" Bijou shouted, stomping her foot and squashing a bent stalk of sugarcane beneath her soft buckled slipper. She turned to leave once more, and looked over her shoulder toward the Kookaburra, who was still laughing and mocking her. "It happens that I *do* know a bird joke!" she began, shouting over the Kookaburra's calling. "What do you call a *rude* bird?" She opened her mouth wide in preparation to answer herself, but the bird beat her to it.

"A *mockingbird!*" he blurted.

Bijou's face turned a blood-red color again. "Oh, *what* an infernal nuisance!" she fumed. She wasn't entirely sure what the phrase meant, but her mother shouted it often at Flora Bell for tracking mud from the neighbor's wet flower beds across the carpet and over their sitting room sofa. She also bellowed it from time to time at the "clumsy newspaper boy," the "lazy milkman," their "nosy neighbor," Mrs. Lord, and quite often at her own "untidy husband." This left Bijou to infer that the phrase was regarded for one's most detested annoyances.

"Could you *at least* tell me which direction the drummer has gone?" Bijou asked impatiently.

"Can you hear the drum *now*?" asked the Kookaburra.

Bijou looked all about frantically, worried that she had missed the drummer, but there was no one. "No," she said shrugging.

"Well, when you *do*, follow it, because *that* will be the direction the drummer is going!" cackled the bird.

Fed up, Bijou spun about on her heels and stomped through the thick sugarcane field, the sound of the Kookaburra's laughter growing more and more faint as she ventured farther away from the pond.

She continued through the swaying sugarcane and came suddenly upon a relieving sight at the bottom of a hill. A lush meadow of giant peonies, which were four times the size of the ones in her mother's garden, lay just before a tall stone tower. The tower had four rotating white wooden blades attached to its front, and they were covered from end to end in twinkling iridescent lights.

"It's a *windmill*!" Bijou exclaimed, darting down the hill and through the meadow.

The windmill had a gilded roof atop its stone tower and a matching arched door at its base. A shallow stream fed a narrow moat, which completely encircled the structure, and Bijou bounded across the water, leaping from one sturdy stepping stone to the next. She hurried to the gilded door and tugged on the giant golden knocker at its center, but the door wouldn't budge.

"Surely, *someone* must live in a place like *this*," she remarked, her eyes tracing a lengthy green vine that snaked up the stone foundation and tower.

It began to coil around one of the descending wooden blades of the windmill, suddenly halting its motion entirely. The inner workings of the windmill began to grumble and moan, the stunted gears sending a thick plume of gray smoke billowing out of the open upper window.

"*Goodness!*" Bijou cried, coughing and waving her hands at the exhaust that now encircled her.

She gripped the edges of two stones and began to scale the tall tower toward its gilded roof. The smoke continued to pour out of the window as Bijou leapt with one determined vault onto the re-strained wooden blade, gripping and jerking the tightening vine as she did. Giving way to her protest, the vine finally snapped, and the blade jutted downward, sending Bijou whipping over the edge and plummeting into the rippling moat below.

"*Goooooooooodneeeeeeeeeess!*"

Thrust deep into the murky moat water, Bijou sank like a stone, disappearing quickly in the muck. She kicked and scrambled toward the surface but continued instead to sink as if she were being pulled under. Half expecting to drown, she was relieved to find herself suddenly spat out the other end of a whirlpool and scooped up into a large red waterwheel. She tumbled downward onto each hard wooden slat with a *thud* and finally fell into a shallow blue pond.

Bijou shivered and studied the familiar waterwheel and pond, sure that she *must* be in her own garden once more. But she quickly realized that this was not her red waterwheel; it was not her garden pond, and it was certainly *not* her yard. The unsettling feeling that she was getting farther away from the nursery instead of closer began to come over her, and Bijou wondered if she'd ever return home, and whether even then if she could be sure that she had.

# Chapter III

## The Tree Dweller's Drum

*Bom-bom, bom-bom!* came the drum from within the Wood.

"Where *are* you?" Bijou grumbled, stomping her foot. Nearly having drowned and now soaking wet, she was no longer in any mood to chase the drum *or* its drummer.

While her stern and persistent mother had tried on many occasions to teach her to swim in the lake near their home, Bijou held closely to her first encounter with the body of water, in which a warm and peaceful autumn lake turned into a chilling winter one that froze solid for months. It seemed to trap all life beneath the surface, and the souls of the fish and creatures hung suspended as they waited for the great thaw of spring. A very small Bijou had decided this to be an evil enchantment placed upon the lake by the Gypsy of the Wood, and there lingered no desire to further trifle with it.

The banyan trees guarded the forest with their sturdy limbs and towering trunks, which stood firm and close to one another, so close that one could hardly see between a row of them. Bijou squinted

her eyes and pursed her lips at the dark forest ahead, and the drum continued its steady beat.

"*Hullo!*" she called. "Are you frightened of me?"

The drum had stopped beating, and no response came.

"I *know* you're here. Beat once for yes and twice for no," Bijou instructed.

*Still* no response came.

"Are you from the Wood?" she persisted.

There was a long pause, and then finally came a sound. *Bom!* The echo of the beat bounced off the giant banyans and back again.

"Do you want to *play*?" Bijou asked, excited once more.

*Bom-bom!* warned the double drumbeat.

Bijou frowned, placing her hands upon her hips. "Then *why* do you beat that drum?" she insisted.

She heard a sound from above, and her eyes followed the distinctive aerial roots of a banyan tree that entangled its enormous trunk from base to bushy top. Bijou imagined that a banyan trunk marked its stature among other trees in the forest, and that their rounded arches were set so high off the ground so that even the tallest and largest beasts in the Wood could walk beneath them without ducking.

Aerial roots shot up from the ground like bamboo rods, and others snaked around neighboring banyan trunks. Bijou had never seen a banyan as tall or grand as the one before her, however, and she stood at the base of the ancient tree searching for a way up.

"I *see* you," she hissed. "I can see your feet, and I can *hear* you breathing."

The Tree Dweller scratched at each bare

ankle with the opposite foot, brushing off patches of dirt before leaping to a higher limb.

In fact, Bijou could see that all of the boy was quite dirty, from his dusty black hair poking from under a brown cap, to his tattered trousers. His fitted jacket was the only article of clothing that seemed his size, and was fastened with four gilded claws, their sharp points hooked through four golden threaded loops. Bijou wondered how a set of beast claws had simply been left about for the boy to find, or if it had been that the *beast* first found the boy. Either scenario was just as intriguing to her.

"I'm coming up!" Bijou shouted, stomping her foot.

*Bom-bom!* came the drum in protest.

"Yes!" she barked back.

*Bom-bom!*

"Yes!"

*Bom-bom!!!*

"*Yes!!!*" Bijou shouted back again, gripping a low branch and pulling herself onto it.

She chased the Tree Dweller up the banyan until he was cornered on its highest limb. The tapping of their steps on the bark rattled a family of black mamo birds, who flew out of their nest, observing the intrusion from high atop the Wood. Bijou was sure the black mamo were extinct, though, admittedly, biology was not her strongest subject, and perhaps it was simply that they *were* extinct in the upper world, but not in the lower Wood.

The Tree Dweller crouched behind the leathery leaves, his drum glowing and illuminating his young face.

"*There* you are!" Bijou called, inching slowly across the branch toward the boy. "I heard your drum, and I followed it here. Only now I'm so far from where I began that I'm afraid I can't find my way back."

"And *what* makes you think you *ought* to?" replied the Tree Dweller smartly, throwing his hands on his hips.

"But I *must* go back *sometime*," she insisted. "Mother and Father will be searching the nursery for me soon. Besides, if the windmill's keeper had been home, I'm sure that I would be home *already*," she added sternly.

"Shows what *you* know," snarked the boy. "Depends on which way the wind blows."

"Doesn't the wind blow the windmill's blades the same direction *every* day?" Bijou asked.

"*Fool* girl!" scoffed the boy. "When the wind changes, does it not blow blades of grass in the opposite direction than it did before?"

"Well, *yes*, but—"

"Then there you have it!" the boy interrupted, smirking smugly.

Bijou rolled her eyes and breathed an exhausted sigh. "Who *are* you, boy?"

"Since you're standing on *my* branch, in *my* tree, don't you think you ought to tell me *your* name first?"

"Of course, where are my manners?" she apologized quickly. "My name is Bijou. Who are *you*?"

"The *Tree Dweller*, of course," he said, dropping his hands to his hips once more in a proud stance despite his filthy appearance.

"Do you mean that you *live* here?"

"*Obviously!*" he snorted, cupping his hands over his mouth as he laughed.

"And *where* are your parents, boy?"

"What are those?"

"Oh *dear!*" Bijou gasped, putting her hand to her wide-open mouth. "If you don't know, then I suppose you haven't any." She thought a boy without parents was an incredibly sad concept, and realized that the Tree Dweller was likely so dirty and impudent because he lived in his tree all alone.

"*Well*, if I don't already know what parents *are* then perhaps I haven't a *need* for them in the first place," said the boy smugly.

By his untidy state, Bijou doubted that very much.

The cocky boy smirked again and congratulated himself on his quick wit as he paced back and forth on the high limb. "What does one use these parents for, anyway?"

"Well, for shelter and supper, I suppose," Bijou offered, though, she knew parents had many other uses, those were just the ones that came immediately to mind.

"But I have my *own* banyan for shelter, and I fetch my own berries and beasts for my own *feasts!*"

"But parents also *love*, boy. Don't you ever get lonely?" Bijou asked, sure that if the boy had ever had a mother, even one as stern as her own, he would certainly miss the scent of her cucumber cold cream, or the sound of her distinct but out-of-tune hum as she tended the garden or baked in the kitchen. Admittedly, Bijou missed those particulars just now.

"What purpose would a *marvelous* boy have to be so lonely? There are many friends and foes in the Wood, and *I* know them all! Any nittidumdum would know *that*."

"Pardon *me!*" Bijou spat, stomping her foot. "You're the one who beat your drum and lured me here from my nursery!"

Bijou turned on her heels and began to climb down the tree as the Tree Dweller hopped to a lower limb with ease and dangled from the branch above by one hand, taunting her.

"*Oh*, what do you want?" she huffed, continuing her descent.

"Do you want your wish, or *don't* you?"

"*Wish*? What wish?" Bijou asked, perking up quickly.

"The one from the fallen star, of course," said the Tree Dweller, smirking and raising an eyebrow. He squatted down before Bijou, pulling at one of her yellow curls until she gave a yelp. "*Everyone* knows that!"

"How would *you* like it if I pulled *your* hair?" she demanded, the Tree Dweller dodging her grasp with ease.

"*Ha!* I'd *dash* you, dull girl! Besides, you'd have to catch me first!" he mocked, jumping quickly from limb to limb.

Bijou chased him up and down the tree, but always seemed to be a few branches behind and eventually gave up, continuing down the banyan.

"You'll never find your fallen star without *my* help!" he bellowed from above her.

"Clearly I wouldn't find it *with* your help either!" she bellowed back.

"It's just *there*, you know," said the Tree Dweller, pointing through the leathery leaves of the banyan and to the top of the mountain toward a set of gilded castle spires. "All you have to do is get there!"

"And *where* is *there*?" Bijou demanded.

"The Gilded Queen's castle, of course! Up Moon Mountain!"

"*Moon Mountain?*" Bijou whispered to herself, thinking of her paper dolls. "That is a *real* place? And the Gilded Queen, *she* is real?"

"You see the gilded castle spires through the Wood, don't you? And where there is a castle, there will surely be a queen, won't there be?" The Tree Dweller hopped down to her branch and tugged again at a yellow curl. "Nittidumdum!"

"But *how* will I get all the way up the mountain and to the castle on my own?" Bijou cried, swatting his hand away again.

The boy stood back, rubbing his chin and examining Bijou. "Well, you don't have wings, so you won't *fly* there. I suppose you'll have to *walk*, won't you? And *if* you find your star you can wish yourself home to these parents of yours." With that the Tree Dweller swung to the next banyan on a pair of thick green vines and back again to the highest limb of his tree, then disappeared.

Bijou climbed as quickly as she could up the tree after him, but once she got to the top again, he had gone.

"*Well*," she huffed, stomping her foot, her eyes beginning to well with tears. But as she stomped her foot on the branch, it made a strange and hollow sound. Bijou looked down between her soft buckled slippers and discovered she was standing on another trap-door. It had a gilded knocker at its center just like the trap beneath her dollhouse, and she tugged on it, lifting the heavy wooden door open.

*Bom-bom, bom-bom!* came the Tree Dweller's drum from inside the ancient banyan. Bijou could hardly believe that all of the places she'd dreamed up for her dolls were real, and she suddenly began to feel uneasy, for she knew that meant the Gilded Queen and her fearsome Black Beast were real too. She gulped nervously and lowered herself into the banyan, and the deep and steady drumbeat sounded again, leading her onward.

# Chapter IV

## The Hidden Home in the Ancient Banyan

Bijou could hardly see but a few inches in front of her inside the dark banyan, and she stretched out her arms to search for a door. All of a sudden, dozens of golden fireflies began to wake and flicker inside of a large glass lantern hanging from the ceiling above her.

"How clever!" Bijou remarked, studying the tiny bugs that were jumping about in the lantern and illuminating the small corridor. "That boy might be dirty, but he's clever," she added.

Bijou eyed the glowing creatures, rubbing her chin as she pondered.

"*My* advice to you," she advised herself, "would be to borrow the boy's lantern. And besides, you can always return it when you see him next." Bijou shook her head, satisfied with her idea, then lifted the lantern from its hook and shone the light on a maroon velvet curtain, lifting it back and unveiling the Tree Dweller's small but cozy home.

She fastened the curtain's golden tie-back rope around two small wooden knots in the trunk and ran her fingers through its shiny tassels that wiggled like golden worms on a hook. They reminded Bijou of her mother's favorite golden lamp in their sitting room at home. She had forbade Bijou to touch it because it was "*very* old and *far* too fragile to be played with by little girls." Of course, this never stopped Bijou from wearing the fringed shade as a crown and pretending to be an Indian princess while her mother worked in their garden. This was her secret game, known only to one other, and that was Flora Bell.

The dark corridor opened up into a small, round room, and there were all manner of knickknacks, totems, swords, and luxurious garments strewn about the narrow abode. At its center was a fire pit made of flat river stones, which had hundreds of small celestial shapes carved into them. The patch of moss atop a pile of logs was suddenly set aflame all on its own, and the glow of the fire shone through the carvings, scattering light in the shapes of moons and stars across the dark ceiling and walls, giving the illusion of an endless night sky. Bijou was sure she'd never seen as many stars in the sky over their lake at home as were now sprinkled about the interior of the banyan trunk. She attempted to count all of them, but kept losing her place when she'd spin about to begin a new cluster. And anyway, there were far too many curious items in the hidden home that commanded her attention.

The small room warmed quickly as Bijou dried herself by the fire, and its smoke rose, funneling through a narrow hole in the banyan's giant trunk. As she looked about, Bijou noticed there was no washroom, though it did not seem that the Tree Dweller washed enough to require one. A wooden slab lay upon two short tree stumps. This, Bijou assumed, was where the Tree Dweller slept, but there was merely a crumpled black fur atop it for a cover, and it occurred to her that the boy did not appear so rested either.

*What good is a place to sleep if one does not?* she thought. If her mother had decided her dollhouse to be a waste of space, she would surely say that a boy who wouldn't go to bed should not have one *at all*.

But Bijou, being a child and *not* a sensible grown-up, had decided that she liked the Tree Dweller's interesting home, despite a few missing pieces of furniture. *And what would be the use of a washroom to a boy who has never washed?* That, she thought, *would* be quite a silly waste of space in a home so small.

Bijou surveyed the small room again, admiring the many swords that hung on a long wall. She marveled at the number of trinkets and medallions that dangled from the ceiling and glistened in the light that poured in from the narrow smoke hole.

"I suppose without any parents to buy him clothes or toys, the boy has to scavenge for things," she remarked to herself, poking timidly at a pin stuck through a small doll that hung on a hook. It muttered something back to her that sounded like a plea to remove the pin, but Bijou didn't dare. There was simply no telling what magic was afoot there.

Bijou spied a closed window in the banyan's trunk and rushed toward it, pushing it open. A thick fog was settling below, and the Tree Dweller was nowhere in sight, but she could suddenly hear the steady beat of his drum once more. She caught a glimmer of the drum's glow bouncing between the banyans below and toward a narrow river that ran alongside the Wood.

"*Oh!*" she grumbled, banging her fist angrily on the windowsill and slamming the trap shut.

Beneath her feet was another small trapdoor in the floor, and Bijou wasted no time throwing it open to peer inside.

"He *is* a clever boy!" she exclaimed, squinting her eyes and trying to see through the darkness below.

Bijou placed the firefly lantern on the floor next to her and summoned her bravery once again, straddling the frame and taking a deep breath. With her arm through the lantern handle, she slipped into the dark chute.

Sliding, sliding, she slid for what seemed like ages down a surface that felt much like sliding down a curved tree trunk or a banister that hadn't been sanded. Bijou's stern mother always knew when she had been sliding, for her dresses and stockings told the tales with tiny rips and tears as evidence. The getting of rips and tears was *always* fun, and while her mother only ever remembered her own added chore of mending, Bijou only ever remembered the *fun*.

She slid *very* slowly down the dark chute, still clinging to the firefly lantern as she went.

"The boy will *surely* reach the castle before *I* do at this rate," she grumbled, attempting to scoot her bottom along faster.

Bijou thought that certainly gravity would have pulled her down quickly, but it was as if it didn't exist inside the chute, and she was going along so slowly that she could have easily been going up and not down.

"Perhaps *that's* why they call it a theory," she pondered aloud. "But of course, Bijou," she began, lecturing herself as her teacher would have from a science book, "gravity *is* powerful enough to hold *people* and bodies of *water* down upon a spinning ball.

But now, let me see, what doesn't it pull down? Well, birds *in flight*, of course, and bees, and other flying bugs. Though, one might argue that birds, bees and other flying bugs are able to fly freely because they use their little wings to push against and through the great force. Then *again*, there are *balloons*, and they haven't any wings at all. And what about *smoke*? Perhaps in *this* chute I'm as light as a balloon or smoke!"

Just as Bijou had begun to consider how wonderful it would be to float about like a balloon and defy all the invisible forces she wanted, she began to slide faster and faster until she could feel the wind of the Wood upon her again.

"*Goodness!*" she exclaimed, clutching her lantern tighter.

All her thoughts of being weightless suddenly left the front of her mind as quickly as her soft buckled slippers neared the mossy ground below. The wind came even more fiercely through the opening in the chute as she fell faster still, and before she knew it, Bijou hit the ground and went tumbling forward into a great and thick fog.

# Chapter V

## The Pygmy Music Makers

Bijou flew out of the dark chute, tumbling and rolling before landing in a patch of giant purple allium bulb flowers. These had always been her favorite flowers because she thought their bulbs looked like pom-pons on long green peppermint sticks. The purple pom-pons swayed in unison, left to right and back again in the wind, releasing a cloud of sticky purple pollen. Bijou began to sneeze uncontrollably, the pollen clinging to her hair and dress like a fungus. She spun around and around, suddenly unable to see through the thick cloud.

"*Goodness!*" she cried, slipping on the dewy moss and down a steep hill onto a sandy bank below. She brushed off the sticky purple pollen and kicked her feet angrily to empty her slippers of sand.

Abandoned on the bank before her was a rickety wooden raft, and she hesitated a moment, eyeing the rushing river water.

*Bom-bom, bom-bom, bom-bom, bom-bom!* came the steady drumbeat once more, and Bijou took a few steps backward, giving herself a running start and then leapt onto the raft.

There were no oars or paddles, so she dipped a finger into the river timidly. Just as she suspected, it was as icy as the lake at home in the winter, but Bijou knew she'd only get downriver quickly one of two ways, paddling or swimming, and she was most certainly *not* going to swim. Using her arm to paddle, Bijou thrust it in and out of the frigid water as quickly as she could, and her raft began to pick up speed as it floated into a great gray fog.

The fog sat low on the river—too low to see beneath it, yet too thick to see around or above. Suddenly, a loud *caw* came from above, and Bijou noticed a flock of black mamo birds flying along with her raft. She could see gleaming sets of yellow eyes that were following her from within the forest, and she wondered if the entire Wood was watching her.

All at once, there came a jolly-sounding ruckus from up ahead. Bijou could hear violins, tambourines, flutes, and trumpets, along with clapping of hands and stomping of feet all around her raft that had suddenly slowed and come to a stop.

"Who are they?" she whispered to herself excitedly, looking all about and straining to see through the relentless fog. "*Oh*, it must be a jamboree!" she cooed.

Bijou could no longer paddle, and the water was now a still and lazy river. Just then, the tip of a wooden canoe became visible through the mist and seemed to be headed directly for her. It was painted the colors of the river, and she knew if she blinked for even a second the mysterious vessel would be lost in the camouflaging water.

"Hulllllooo?" she called out, but no response came.

Her raft was now surrounded by a crew of canoes, and a tiny, wrinkled hand reached through the thick fog toward her. Little by little, more of the mysterious person became visible. A cloaked arm became an entire cloaked and hooded pygmy, and she could see nothing more of him than a set of bright green eyes peeking out from under his giant hood. This reminded Bijou of how Flora Bell would hide under her bed and leap out to paw at her bare feet. He often attempted this game with her stern mother as well, and afterward would come a slew of phrases which Bijou could never quite understand. Flora Bell, however, would insist that he *could* understand and *always* seemed pleased with himself.

The short stranger hopped suddenly from his boat and onto Bijou's raft, and he crouched down, looking all about cautiously. As he stood upright, Bijou could see that he came just below her waist and appeared swallowed up by his oversized cloak. He stood silently, as if waiting for her to speak first.

"Excuse me, s-sir," she stammered, "but, could you tell me how to get to the Queen's castle? I seem to have lost my guide and—"

"I am *not* a *ssssir*. I am called *Pygmy*, and the Tree Dweller *isssssn't* your *guide*," said the Pygmy in a slow and drawn-out manner.

The stranger sounded like a hissing snake, or what Bijou thought a snake might sound like if it could talk.

"You're meant to chasssssse the drum, you know," he added.

"*Clearly*," Bijou whispered to herself.

"Perhaps *thisssss* will help once you get there," hissed the Pygmy, pulling a miniature golden flute from inside the oversized sleeve of his cloak and placing it in Bijou's hand.

"For *me*?" she gasped. "Should I play it for the Queen?"

"Sssssssssstupid girl, *no*! You will need it if you are to get past the Queen's beassssst," he whispered, cupping his hands around his mouth and ordering his crew to play louder so no other creature in the Wood could hear what he was about to say.

"Do you mean the *Black* Beast?" Bijou asked.

"Isssss there another?" he hissed impatiently. "The flute will lull the Black Beast into a deep sssssssssslumber, so take care *not* to drop it!"

"Does the Black Beast *guard* the Queen?" asked Bijou.

"Sssssstupid, stupid girl!" hissed the Pygmy again, leaping back into his canoe. "It guards the tall tower!"

"But what would *I* want with the tall tower?" Bijou shouted back, standing up on her raft and holding her lantern out to see through the fog once more.

"How do you exxxxxxpect to get home?" asked the Pygmy, his voice echoing through his cupped hands.

Bijou thought for a moment, realizing she hadn't told him that she was trying to get home. "But how did *you* know—"

"*Sssssshhhhhhush!*" he whispered angrily. "Can't you see all of the Wood is watching? Besides, the water is awfully black and foul today. Ssssssome wretch must have trifled with it."

"I assure you it wasn't *I!*" Bijou snapped defensively, crossing her arms over her chest.

"We shall ssssssssssee." The Pygmy winked at Bijou and pointed in the direction of the mountain ahead. "*Do* beware the Beast's clawsssssss, sssssstupid girl, for they could ssssssslice you into bits!" He winked each green eye at her once more as he sank into his canoe and rowed away quickly.

Bijou turned about on her raft, realizing the remaining crew had also gone and that the jolly ruckus had stopped.

"What a *peculiar* little creature," she remarked to herself, placing the gilded flute inside her dress pocket. Her raft suddenly jutted forward, and she continued to paddle through the black river with her arm, this time faster for fear of why the water was *foul*.

Bijou soon came upon a rocky beach at the base of Moon Mountain, and she gathered the soaked raft ropes that she'd carelessly allowed to drag in the water for the entirety of her journey. She tied loops at their ends and tossed them around a tree stump on the river bank, then pulled herself to shore. The rushing water yanked at the raft, unraveling the poorly tied loops, and her rickety vessel began to float swiftly downriver.

"Oh *no*! Wait, *please* wait!" Bijou cried, rushing to grab the ropes, but she stopped suddenly and cringed, realizing her blunder. "Of course I can't row *up* a rushing river to get home," she scolded herself, feeling quite like a stupid girl, indeed.

She held her lantern up once more, and even with a blazing sun far above her, the Wood was so dark that the trickle of light her lantern gave only illuminated a few steps ahead of her on the winding trail. The dark Wood gave her dark feelings, and Bijou began to worry about the Black Beast and the tower it guarded. She wondered what other daydreams she thought she'd only ever imagined might just be real.

# Chapter VI

## The Great Auk Potter and the Sweetie Maker Herself

Bijou came upon a canopy of towering purple jacaranda trees. They completely surrounded a small stone cottage, which had a garden-lined pathway that led to an arched wooden door. Its thatched roof was a light shade of sierra, while a rich and inviting forest-green ivy grew over the stone wall exterior. The shutters were wide open, and Bijou could smell the scent of something delicious baking inside. As she stood sniffing the air, a strong grip suddenly encircled her waist, scooping her into the crook of a large wing.

"My dear, *there* you are!" came a raspy voice from above her.

An old great auk in a smart bowler hat, violet vest, and brown plaid jacket and trousers, hurried up the stone walk and plunked Bijou down in front of the arched door. The giant bird, with a black head and beak, and body with coloring similar to that of a penguin, reached for the giant golden door knocker, rapping it three times.

"I should *think* a person invited to supper with the Sweetie

Maker would graciously attend *on time*," he scoffed, checking one of ten small pocket watches that hung from his jacket and vest.

"Pardon *me!*" Bijou snapped. "But I'm not accustomed to being gallivanted around under the wing of a complete stranger!" For a moment Bijou had to think about what she'd just said, realizing it was just as ridiculous as talking to a giant bird in the first place. But then, she *had* already spoken to one bird in the Wood, and everything and *everyone* thus far *had* been ridiculous.

"Stranger? *Humph!*" scoffed the giant bird. "*I* am the Great Auk Potter! Now we are not strangers," he added smartly, smirking and rapping at the door again as he checked the time impatiently.

His pocket watches were different sizes, colors and shapes, and they fascinated Bijou. She had always been fascinated with her father's pocket watch because it had a beautiful engraving of a grand elephant behind the big and little hands. He'd traded a worn copy of his favorite book of poetry for the watch, which had belonged to a Bohemian of Bombay. Bijou didn't know where that was, but from the sound of her father's wild stories, it seemed a magical place—a place where they kept elephants and Bohemians, anyway.

"Why do you have so many?" she asked, eyeing the Auk's timepieces.

"How shall I tell the time otherwise?"

"Can't you tell time with *one,* or perhaps just a few?"

"Ha!" he scoffed. "Shows what *you* know about time, my dear. *A few* will not *do* at all! Besides, *I* know a word of letters *three*, add two, and *fewer* there shall *be!*"

Bijou pondered the riddle for a moment.

The Auk tapped his webbed foot impatiently.

"The word is *few!*" she answered proudly, sticking her chin up into the air.

"Of course it is!" spat the Auk, unimpressed. "Besides, I need multiple watches because the time is different for every *different place* that I go," he added. "*Everyone* knows that!"

All of a sudden, the arched door flew open, and the guests were met by a short, portly woman in a flour-dusted apron and a stark-white poplin chef's hat that flopped to one side like an oversized melted marshmallow.

"*There* you are!" she shrieked, wrenching the pair one at a time through the archway and slamming the door shut.

She thrust Bijou into a large red-and-white striped armchair, which reminded her of the giant circus tent she'd wandered through one night after cleverly and quietly slipping away from her mother while she was in conversation. Bijou had eagerly toured all of the back halls of that tent. She had roamed through all of the private compartments of every caboose in the train. She had spied on the clowns practicing their bits, and then on the armless woman, who was applying her show make-up with her toes. Bijou had decided that the lives of those traveling performers must be simply fantastic, and she vowed to remain lost under that tent and to run away with the circus—that is, until her mother finally discovered her attempting to set free the trained tigers from their cramped cages. Bijou's heart ached for the poor beasts, and she had merely wanted to let them out for a bit to play freely. Her stern mother swore right then and there that the evening would be the *last* circus outing for the mischievous child. And it had been.

"Now, sit there and mind yourself, sugar," the Sweetie Maker instructed, fumbling with her floppy hat.

She turned quickly on her heels and threw open the oven door, the scent of something delectable wafting toward Bijou. And though Bijou didn't actually have time to stop for a bite, she was much too exhausted, and suddenly very hungry, to protest.

The Sweetie Maker whipped a hot sheet of plump golden jelly rolls from the top rack, sliding them onto a three-tiered silver serving tray. Bijou eyed them, and her mouth dropped open. The sweeties were even more scrumptious-looking than the ones her mother made on Sundays, though, she would never dare say so.

All about the cozy kitchen were piles of plum pies, towers of thimble-berry teacakes, and endless trays of pink tayberry tarts.

"Do you care for jelly rolls?" asked the Auk.

Bijou nodded eagerly, her eyes as large as the tarts and teacakes themselves. She reached out to take a roll, which was oozing the most scrumptious-looking sugar-pear and wild-berry filling from its spiral ends.

"*You* have not been invited!" the Sweetie Maker tisked, smacking Bijou's hand away with a rolling pin from her apron.

"*Quite*," agreed the Auk, smearing a generous layer of purple pumpernickel jam on a freshly baked banana-berry biscuit.

"Well, I *beg* your pardon, but the bird asked if I'd care for one!" Bijou barked, jumping out of her seat and slapping both palms down on the tabletop.

"I didn't ask if you'd care for one; I merely asked if you cared for jelly rolls," replied the Auk nonchalantly.

Bijou grumbled angrily and eyed the rude bird. "*You* haven't even introduced yourself, you know," she pointed out, crossing her arms over her chest and sulking.

"Well, neither have *you*, sugar," the Sweetie Maker scolded. She poured herself another cup of tea from a large silver teapot. "Thimble-berry tea goes well with a sweetie, does it not?"

"I *wouldn't* know!" Bijou snapped, stomping her foot and turning to leave.

"*I* am the Sweetie Maker, and *you*, sugar, are in the cottage of the Sweetie Maker *herself*."

Bijou turned back and placed her hands in her dress pockets as she stood and watched the portly woman guzzle every last drop of her tea.

"*I* make all the pots, pans, bottles and ale steins that she needs. It *is* my business, you know," the Auk whispered to Bijou, poking her side with his wing.

"Well, *my* name is Bijou," she replied, seating herself again in the striped armchair.

"What a peculiar thing to be called," the Sweetie Maker chuckled. "Would you care for a sweetie or a sip, sugar?"

"Perhaps a glass of lemonade?" Bijou asked, suddenly parched from all the arguing.

"What in *nittination* is that?" scoffed the Sweetie Maker.

"Well, you make it with lemons and sugar water, of course," Bijou replied.

"You're *mad* as *Mer*! The water is no good to drink! *Everyone* knows that," mocked the Sweetie Maker. "But *do* try a sip of my Hot Holland Cocoa, and tell me what you think!" The Sweetie Maker nudged the Auk, winking at him as she guzzled another cup of tea, and Bijou wondered what the tea could possibly be made from if it had no water in it. She then realized that she didn't really want to know.

The Auk pulled a blue and white stein from beneath his perfectly rounded hat and filled it with cocoa from a large jug at the center of the table. He then took his brown corncob pipe from his vest pocket and began tapping it upside down on the kitchen table, its contents spilling out before he started to pack it once more.

*How awful*, Bijou thought, cringing. She never liked it when her father smoked his pipe indoors. It had the most awful, skunky stench, which she and her stern mother couldn't abide at all.

The Sweetie Maker suddenly lurched forward to pluck a whisker from beside the nose of her black cat, who had pounced onto the table. She had patches of white flour dust all over her fur and was licking madly at it while sneezing and blowing it back onto herself again.

*Poor darling*, Bijou thought, shaking her head.

"*Down*, Jellybean!" the Sweetie Maker ordered, flicking the whisker into a boiling concoction on the stove top.

Bijou grimaced, shifting nervously in her chair. The black cat reminded her of Flora Bell, and she would *never* have treated *him* so badly.

The Sweetie Maker hissed at the cat and continued stirring her concoction with a giant wooden spoon.

"Now, where are you journeying to, my dear?" asked the Auk, taking a puff from his pipe, a gray smoke ringlet encircling his nose before dissipating into the air.

"The castle," Bijou replied nonchalantly, taking a sip of the Hot Holland Cocoa and gagging on the strong, spicy taste. It suddenly seemed to give her added energy. Her eyes opened wide, and her fingers began to drum involuntarily on the table as her feet fidgeted about on the floor.

"The *castle!*" cried the Sweetie Maker and Auk in unison.

"What business do *you* have with the *wretch?*" the Auk insisted.

"Why do you call the Queen *wretch?*" Bijou asked, setting her heavy stein back on the table and wiping the cocoa foam from her mouth.

"She *is* one, you know!" spat the Sweetie Maker, turning on her heels again and stirring her concoction angrily. "*Voilà!*" she bellowed, heaving her pot into the air with satisfaction. "Bottle, Potter," she instructed the Auk.

The Auk plunged a wing into his jacket pocket and fished out various-sized bottles until he came upon an unmarked glass vial.

"Ah-*ha!*" he exclaimed, steadying the vial while the Sweetie Maker filled it with her concoction.

"Take this potion to the wretch, sugar, and tell her it's from *me!*" said the Sweetie Maker, smiling a satisfied smile.

"But you already had that pot boiling when I came in," Bijou remarked.

"*Yes?*" the Sweetie Maker insisted.

"Well, it's as if you'd been expecting me."

"You *see?* I *told* you that you'd been *invited,*" replied the Auk smugly, corking the vial and tucking it into Bijou's dress pocket.

"Oh, *what* an infernal nuisance!" Bijou grumbled, leaping to her feet again and marching toward the arched door, the flour-dusted black cat in tow.

"Wait!" pleaded the Sweetie Maker. "Don't forget to give her the potion!"

"But you haven't even told me what this potion will do!" Bijou insisted, stomping her foot.

"How should *I* know, sugar?"

"But *you* made the potion just now," Bijou spat. "Don't you remember what it does?"

"Of course not!" the Sweetie Maker scolded, tapping Bijou on the head with her rolling pin. "I am much too busy to bother with what each potion *does!*"

Bijou growled angrily at the idiotic pair and spun about again, marching out of the Sweetie Maker's cottage.

The poor black cat attempted its escape but bumped its head into the arched door as it slammed shut, and the Sweetie Maker merely hissed at it again. The desperate cat leapt out of the high open window and then disappeared up a jacaranda tree, watching Bijou as she walked.

Bijou scooped up her lantern and hurried down the stone pathway as the sugary aroma of freshly baked pastries and sweeties began to fade from her senses. She continued again up the mossy trail of the mountain, her energy from the Hot Holland Cocoa wearing off and leaving her with a slight buzzing in her ears.

"What *next?*" she grumbled to herself, attempting to shake the buzzing out of her head and cursing the cocoa as she went.

# Chapter VII

## Sold to the Gypsies

As Bijou continued up the mountain, she came upon a small golden music box nestled in a patch of daisies.

"How careless of someone. Mother gave me a box *just* like this," she remarked, kneeling down and lifting its hinged lid. "Should it play the same tune as *your* music box," she began to herself, "then perhaps *you* dropped it." Bijou smiled proudly, congratulating herself on her cleverness, even if she knew full well that she hadn't dropped it. Still, she hoped that no one would come to claim it anyway.

Bijou wound the tiny key on the side of the gilded box a few turns, and the brass combs inside began to pluck the notes on the pin drum. A familiar and soothing melody began to pling and plong, and she suddenly felt very tired. She yawned and stretched, picking one of the yellow daisies from the patch as she sank to the mossy ground. While listening to the soft song and twirling the daisy about between her fingers, Bijou quickly drifted off to sleep.

"Wake up, girl, wake up!" came a shrill voice.

A silver-haired old woman stood above Bijou wearing a black corseted dress, which was covered in gold and silver coins. Her hair was wrapped in a red silk scarf, and on her frail arms she wore bands of silver bangles that slinked up and down as she moved. The woman jingled as she swayed her hips back and forth, and the brilliant sapphires adorning her forehead sparkled and slid up and down as she winked both dark eyes at Bijou.

Behind the woman was a small wooden caravan that had a gilded arched roof and door, and where Bijou was sure there would normally have been a horse or even a pony to pull a caravan, there instead stood a pair of Falkland warrah wolves. Their fur was a muddy brown, except for a patch of white under their necks and at the ends of their bushy tails, and they stood only two feet tall. They each wore bands of jewels, beads and silver coins around their necks like the old woman, and even their eyelids were adorned with sapphires.

"Wake up, *lazy* girl!" barked the old woman once more.

"I *am* awake!" Bijou shouted back, rubbing her tired eyes. "You shouldn't *bellow* at people while they're sleeping!" she scolded, wagging her finger at the old woman.

"And *lazy* little girls shouldn't go about *napping* in other people's daisy patches, let alone *picking* one of the little dears!" the old woman snapped, smirking as she danced about Bijou idiotically.

"*Your* daisy patch? That's ridiculous!" Bijou pouted, sticking her chin into the air. "They don't belong to *you*. I could pick one or *many* if I wanted."

"Listen here, *lazy* girl," the woman began, whirling about and peering down at Bijou with her hypnotic eyes. "Do *not* mistake a wildflower for a garden rose, though, at times it mistakes itself. It cannot be kept, even if desired to be. For you see, the *wild* will sabotage itself to be *free*."

The old woman snatched the yellow daisy from between Bijou's fingers and buried it quickly in the mossy ground. Bijou watched the patch of moss for a moment, and a green sprout suddenly began to peek through the moss and bloomed into another daisy right before her eyes.

"Now, *what* is your purpose in *my* daisy patch, child?"

"Well," Bijou gulped, "I found this music box in the patch, and—"

"*There* it is!" the old woman bellowed, snatching the box out of Bijou's hand. "I thought I'd sold this to a traveling gypsy! Or, at least I'd meant to," she trailed off, tapping her chin in thought.

"Pardon me, but why would you sell it?" Bijou began. "It seems like such a lovely music box, and I have one just—"

"This piece of *junk*?" blurted the woman. "I wager you would trade anything for this worthless box," she mocked, waving it back and forth.

"It *isn't* junk!" Bijou demanded. "But anyway, I have nothing to trade for it."

"*Oh*, but you *do*. The Pygmy's flute will do just nicely."

"How did you—"

"I know *all*, child. *I* am Madam Loulou de la Mer, the gypsy fortune-teller of this Wood."

"Doesn't mer mean *sea*?"

"Aren't you *clever*?" the gypsy condescended. "I am *come* from the sea, but I am the teller of fortunes in the Wood. We *all* dwell in caravans along the river or by the sea, and even *on* the sea, but it's quite crowded there, you see?"

"Well, Madam—"

"*Mer*," chimed the gypsy.

"Madam *Mer*," Bijou repeated. "I *can't* give you this flute. I have to use it to lull the Queen's Black Beast to sleep."

"That *wretch*?" shrieked Madam Mer. "If *you* are a friend to the wretch, then I think I'll sell you to the gypsies *next*!"

"You will *not* sell *me*!" Bijou scoffed, throwing her hands on her hips. "Besides, I am no friend of the wretch—I mean, the *Queen*," she corrected herself, blushing. "Why does everyone call her—," Bijou stopped to cup one hand around her mouth and began to whisper, "*wretch*?"

"Ha!" Madam Mer cackled, grabbing her stomach and bowling over with laughter as she poked at Bijou's ruffled sleeve with her slender and bejeweled finger. "Listen here, child—"

"*Bijou* is my name!" she snapped sternly.

Madam Mer straightened up and thought for a moment. "That means *jewel*, you know," she replied matter-of-factly, poking at Bijou's nose condescendingly. "Where are you headed, little jewel? *I'm* on my way to the Queendom."

"The *Queendom*?" Bijou repeated, never having heard it put that way before. "Don't you mean *Kingdom*?"

"But there *isn't* a king," said Madam Mer, wagging her bejeweled finger. "And if there is only a queen, then her dominion should be a *queendom*, should it not?"

"I *suppose*," Bijou sighed, rolling her eyes.

Madam Mer took a step toward Bijou and sniffed the air. "*You* smell of river water," she remarked, pinching her nose between her finger and thumb and grimacing.

Bijou's mouth fell open and her cheeks turned blood-red. "Nothing of the sort!" she exclaimed angrily, never having liked being embarrassed or poked fun at.

Bijou sniffed the air about her and furrowed her brow slightly, realizing that there was an odd odor. "Well, if I *do* smell of river water, it's merely because I *have* been in the river today!"

"And a few *ponds* too," Madam Mer added, wrinkling her nose at Bijou and waving her hand in disgust. "Don't you know swimming in the river is forbidden?"

"I wasn't *swimming*. I fell!" Bijou barked. "And anyway, how*ever* could swimming be forbidden? Not that I *can* swim," she added, a bit embarrassed again.

"There is an enchantment on the water of the Wood, you know," Madam Mer warned. "I should know, *I* placed it there!"

"*That's* why the water is no good to drink!" Bijou began. "Why would you poison the water?"

"Who said it was poisoned?" Madam Mer snapped. "I simply altered the taste somewhat, and, perhaps, the *effect!*" She began to roar with laughter once more, spinning about idiotically.

"What do you mean, '*effect?*'" Bijou demanded, slightly worried that something awful might now happen to her. *Perhaps that's why the water is foul,* she thought, cringing.

"Let's take a look, shall we?" said Madam Mer, clutching Bijou's hand and yanking her under the arched door of her caravan and pulling her inside.

The caravan suddenly seemed to open up like an accordion, and the room began to expand before Bijou's very eyes. Its walls were gold-gilded, and the floor-to-ceiling cabinets and compartments were painted a deep royal blue. Sitting atop each surface were shimmering crystal balls and clusters of white candles that suddenly lit themselves at the snap of the old woman's fingers. Their flickering lights began to reflect off of the gilded mirrors that hung on every inch of spare wall, and all of the beautiful things inside the caravan became illuminated.

Bijou felt somewhat hypnotized, and she swore she could hear a faint call for help. She looked all about, finally spying a trapped little man inside a tall glass bottle on a shelf. He wore a black top-hat and tuxedo, and he banged furiously on the glass with both fists.

"Never mind that," said Madam Mer, flinging Bijou into a pile of brightly colored silk cushions.

Madam Mer snapped her fingers again, and as she did, a small table suddenly appeared before Bijou, and the old woman took her place at the other end.

"Give me your palm, child, and I'll read your fortune," she purred, squinting her dark eyes and grinning slightly.

Bijou placed her hand on top of Madam Mer's, palm upward, and spoke not a word. She had heard stories of the traveling carnival gypsies who offer to tell one's fortune for a few coins, but as she didn't have any coins, Bijou thought it wise to remain silent on the matter.

Madam Mer began to scrutinize Bijou's palm meticulously, yanking and twisting it about as she squinted and let out the occasional grunt. "*Just* as I suspected," she began, looking up at Bijou and smirking.

"What? What is it?" Bijou asked nervously.

Madam Mer released Bijou's hand and sat back into her cushions. "*You* are a *very* curious child," she remarked, drumming her fingers on the table, seeming pleased with herself.

"Is that *all?*" Bijou demanded, staring at the lines of her palm.

"Well, that says a great deal about a child who finds herself lost in the Wood and swimming in enchanted waters, don't you think?"

The old woman leapt up from her comfortable cushions and flew to a tall wall of random treasures and junk. The clutter had small perfume bottles nestled in here and there, and each one was different from the next, and they all had golden labels fixed to them.

Madam Mer rubbed her chin, tapping it twice, then snapped her fingers again. "Ah-*ha!*" she exclaimed, summoning a small scarlet bottle from a high shelf with the tips of her fingers.

Bijou watched in disbelief as it floated down to the gypsy, landing gently in her palm, and the old woman whirled around and returned to the small table, taking her place again atop her silk cushions.

Bijou carefully examined the small perfume bottle and its label. "Purple *Prying* Potion?" she read aloud suspiciously.

"Yes, this will curb a curious child's prying, peeping, and pestering for a time. Not to mention, dispense of that awful river stench," said Madam Mer, grimacing and waving her hand about her nose. "This should do it," she assured, giving the purple atomizer three quick squeezes.

The sweet-smelling cloud of purple perfume burst into Bijou's eyes and nose, and she began to sneeze uncontrollably once more.

Madam Mer snapped her fingers, and the small scarlet bottle floated quickly back to its high shelf.

"Now, child, I haven't got *all* day," she trailed off, clutching

Bijou's hand again and yanking her out into the Wood while she continued to sneeze and rub her eyes free of the sticky purple mist.

The gypsy taunted Bijou with the golden music box again, and then placed it in her hands. "I have a proposition for you," she began. "I'll tell you the shortcut to the castle, and I'll *lend* you this old music box if you bring it back to me with the Queen *inside!*"

"*Inside?*" Bijou exclaimed, her mouth dropping open once more.

"Yes, I imagine the little wretch will be quite comfortable." Madam Mer touched her finger to Bijou's chin, forcing her mouth shut.

"But *how* shall I manage such a thing?" Bijou demanded. "A wretch she may be, but one does not just put a *queen* inside of a music box!"

The gypsy interlaced their arms and began to pace back and forth, dragging Bijou along.

"Just twist the golden key a few turns, and the box will do the rest," she assured. "Now, you ought to be off. It'll be getting dark very soon, and I should warn you of the tree spirits."

"What are *they?*" Bijou asked, taking a seat on the soft mossy trail and flaring her scarlet dress about her.

Madam Mer knelt down, her rickety knees cracking as she did. "Well, my little jewel, with regard to lore, one is warned *not* to daydream upon sundown in the Wood. Can you guess why?"

"I couldn't *possibly*," Bijou scoffed. "Sounds silly to me."

"I suppose you've *seen* a tree spirit then?" Madam Mer snapped.

"Well, *no*, but—"

"Then I'll continue!" The old woman straightened up and slinked toward the nearest banyan tree. She peered down a deep knothole in its trunk and glanced back over her shoulder at Bijou. "The tree spirits of the ancient banyans have the power to transport a daydreamer to the place where their daydreams live. And while that may seem grand, once you go through a daydream door, it's been told that you don't *ever* come back!"

Her shrill voice flew down the knothole and through the tree, and Bijou was sure that had there actually *been* a tree spirit inside, it would have surely moved on after such an assault.

"That's *preposterous*," Bijou argued, crossing her arms over her chest. "Who ever heard of a *daydream door?*"

"*Furthermore*," barked Madam Mer, "no man alive who has not first daydreamed at sundown has ever set eyes on the curious creatures. Well, they are quite small, you know."

"Tree spirits and daydream doors," Bijou mocked under her breath. She watched the gypsy as she sang and danced idiotically. *The old woman is mad*, she thought to herself. *Mad as a wet hen, as Mother would say.* Bijou had never quite understood why the wet state of the hen angered it so, but after spending part of the day smelling of pond and river water herself, she had begun to sympathize with the poor animal.

"Now, my little jewel, I've a teatime with a pygmy, and I mustn't be late." Madam Mer spun about on her heels abruptly and danced idiotically back to her gilded caravan. She gave each bejeweled wolf a pat on the head and hopped atop the high wooden seat.

"How is it that such small wolves can pull your caravan?" Bijou asked.

"I suppose a child of *your* size can't do anything at all on your own," the gypsy mocked, giving an initial tug on the reins.

"They look awfully tired and hungry to *me*," Bijou muttered, reaching out to pet them.

"Nonsense, they eat every hour," Madam Mer assured.

"That's far too much!" Bijou gasped. "You're *overfeeding* the poor beasts!"

"*Ah*, but the wolf within that *wins* is the one you *feed*," the gypsy whispered, winking at Bijou again and giving another stern tug on the reins. As she did, the wolves lurched forward and darted up the mossy green trail of the mountain. "Do not forget our bargain, or I'll sell you to the gypsies, *lazy* girl!"

"But you never told me why everyone calls the Queen *wretch, or* the shortcut to the castle!"

"Up Moon Mountain is the way, little jewel! You may follow me *if* you can keep up!" Madam Mer cackled and slapped the reins again, then disappeared up the winding trail.

Bijou grumbled to herself, stomping her foot angrily. *Mad as a wet hen!*

She slipped the golden music box inside her pocket and grasped the handle of her firefly lantern. As Bijou passed beneath a dark canopy of entangled banyan branches, she began to feel uneasy again. For an eerie moment, she imagined the tiny tree spirits staring back at her, and she wondered if they were waiting for the sun to set, and for her to daydream.

# Chapter Seven and One Half

# The Phoenix and the Baobab Tree

A giant winged thing lifted off from its perch, suddenly having spotted prey on the mossy ground far below. Descending rapidly and dodging the banyan canopies, the creature extended its talons, clutching Bijou in its secure grasp and lifting back into the air once more.

The Phoenix, with its feathers of a peacock, scales of a reptile, and sunken black eyes, soared through the sky, its catch writhing and wrestling below. What a treat for its young, who were waiting in their nest for a late lunch.

Bijou kicked and howled at the Phoenix, pleading to be dropped. She suddenly came loose from the sharp talons of the monster and plummeted downward, landing in a crowded and noisy straw nest high in a baobab tree. The Phoenix nuzzled its infants and flew off again to fetch them further nourishment.

Unlike any tree Bijou had ever seen, the baobab's bloated and bare trunk stretched high into the sky with only a small patch of bushy green leaves and branches at its very top. She peered over the edge of the nest, frightened and dizzy at the great height, while the newborns chirped and clucked amongst their still unhatched, soon-to-be siblings asleep in their giant gilded eggs.

"I've never seen such giant bird eggs before! I bet I could fit inside one!" Bijou poked at one of the golden eggs as something began to shift about inside it, causing the egg to shudder.

The newborns continued to chirp their warnings at Bijou in between gobbling down piles of worms and slugs.

"*Hullo*, little chicks! Now, I want nothing to do with your lunch. I j-just want to get home in one piece!" Bijou stammered, backing away from the newborns until she found herself at the edge of the nest once more.

The newborns pecked and chirped in her direction, and Bijou began fishing through her pockets for something to give them. She found the glass apothecary bottle marked *Elephant's Wisdom* that she'd taken from the gilded burrow, and she wondered what it might do to the poor chicks if she let them drink it. It occurred to her to drink it herself, though she had the same apprehension.

"Let me see," Bijou began, tapping her chin in thought. "What do you suppose a concoction marked *Elephant's Wisdom* would do, chicks?" She held the small bottle up to them as if she were at the front of a class giving a lecture.

The newborns shook their heads from side to side, for of course, they didn't know.

"An elephant is *very* wise, of course," Bijou went on, straightening up and lowering her voice to mimic her school teacher. "Therefore, we must logically conclude that this concoction shall make its drinker more the wiser!" Certain of her cleverness, Bijou removed the cork and took a sip from the bottle. She swished the concoction about in her mouth for a moment, but nothing happened. "*Hm*," she moaned, thinking to herself. "Perhaps I didn't drink enough of it." Bijou finished the bottle this time, but still nothing happened.

*Chirp, chirp!* warned the newborns, motioning for Bijou to turn around.

She glanced over her shoulder and saw that the Phoenix was returning to the nest with a mouthful of worms and slugs.

"Oh *no*! If only I could fly *too*!" Bijou cried, ducking behind the wall of the nest to hide from the giant monster. "Hold on, that's *it*!" she exclaimed. "What good is a concoction that makes its drinker wiser if the drinker doesn't *think* something wise?"

Bijou stood up and climbed atop the edge of the nest to address her class. "It would be quite wise to wish for *wings*, chicks!"

All at once, a great rumbling was felt from teeth to toes as a pair of iridescent wings suddenly sprouted from her shoulder blades.

"*Goodness!*" she cried, having just enough time to grab her lantern and wave goodbye to the newborns before she was lifted out of the monster's nest.

The newborns chirped their goodbyes as the tired Phoenix returned with more food. It didn't have time to wonder where its catch had gone, for the afternoon had already been far too busy with so many newborns and more on the way for the poor, tired monster to wonder instead of work.

Bijou looked all about as she glided on a wind. She could see all of the places she'd been already, and a few places she hadn't in the distance. Three golden and glistening castle spires began to come more sharply into view, and Bijou flapped her arms to give her wings more speed.

"I think I'll *fly* to the castle after all, boy!" she mocked, recalling how the Tree Dweller had scrutinized her.

As she flew, a dark and seemingly villainous figure carrying a giant golden bow appeared in the Wood far below. He drew back on it and fired a gilded arrow into the sky toward her.

"*Gooooooooooodneeeeeeeeeess!*" she cried, the arrow's sharp tip piercing one of her glistening wings and sending her into a downward spiral. As Bijou crashed through the high branches of the baobabs, she realized that she was spiraling quickly toward the villain himself.

# Chapter VIII

## The Giant Moa Bird and
## His Burlap Sack

Bijou plummeted downward, passing by perched families of curious black mamo birds as she crashed through the branches of the baobab trees. She landed in a pile of loose hay near a stable and a striped gray stag, tumbled out, then dusted off her scarlet dress and patted her wild mane of yellow curls. Bijou reached back to feel for her wings, but they had gone.

"*Oh!*" she bellowed, kicking the ground and crossing her arms over her chest. "What an utter waste of wisdom and cleverness!"

She bent over and turned herself upside down to examine the strange stag beside her. He stood rocking back and forth on the edges of his gilded horseshoes, and he eyed Bijou, mirroring her glances and expressions.

"Peculiar," Bijou remarked nonchalantly, feeling as if she'd seen stranger things thus far. She traced the stag's perfectly straight white stripes with her finger.

The stag didn't mind, for he rarely had visitors to pay him any mind at all.

"You there!" came a deep voice from behind her.

Bijou whirled around, and her eyes followed the large, feathery body of a nine-foot-tall bird that towered over her. The giant bird wore patch-covered trousers belted with a tattered rope over his bushy brown torso feathers. The strap of a worn burlap sack was slung around his long neck and over his back, and a crumpled newspaper was tucked into the crook of one raised leg as he balanced on the other. He flung his burlap sack from around his back and tossed it to the ground, tucking his newspaper inside. The bird stood staring wide-eyed at Bijou, and she stared right back.

"Have you plummeted from your nest, chick?" he asked, peering down at her.

"I'm not a *bird*," Bijou replied sternly. "I'm a *girl*."

"How *unordinary*!" the bird gasped excitedly.

"I believe you mean '*extraordinary*,'" Bijou corrected.

"Why? Do you think you are *extra ordinary*?" he quipped.

Bijou rolled her eyes, too exhausted from her flight and flapping to argue.

"*I* have never heard of a *girl bird*," he continued. "*I* am a *wildfowl*. The *Giant Moa Bird*, uh, to be precise," he stammered.

"*Oh*, did you fall from *your* nest?" Bijou asked.

"*Preposterous*," he scoffed. "Moa are flightless. You see, I haven't wings, only limbs," he pointed out, gesturing toward his thin and gangly legs.

"Pardon me," Bijou began, changing the subject, "but, could you tell me—"

"Shouldn't we be introduced?" the Giant Moa blurted, stretching his long neck and head to within an inch of Bijou's.

"My name is Bijou," she said, outstretching her hand to the bird.

"You are a *giant*?"

"The Giant *Moa*," he corrected, lifting a leg to shake her hand with his foot. "A wayfarer, a wanderer. I packed my sack, no more I sat, and, I roam, no *home* to speak of," he recited, burying his head inside his burlap sack suddenly. He wrestled inside of it for a moment, then surfaced with a small gilded hand mirror clenched tightly in his large beak.

"A *wayfarer*? Like a gypsy?" Bijou asked.

"*P-posterous!*" he mumbled, still clenching the mirror in his beak as he spoke. "Ha' ooo er *'een* a 'ypsy?"

"*Pardon?*" asked Bijou, wondering if her ears were still ringing from the Hot Holland Cocoa.

The Giant Moa removed the mirror from his mouth and stuck it in the crook of his raised leg. "I *said*, have you ever *seen* a gypsy?"

"*Oh!* In fact, I *have*," she replied. "She gave me this music box to trap the *Queen* inside!" Bijou pulled the box from her dress pocket to show him.

"*Marvelous* idea!" he proclaimed, tapping her on the head with the end of his mirror. "Come!" he shouted, plucking Bijou up by the back of her dress collar and dropping her in a seated position on the tall pile of hay. "Are you lost? Where would you like to go?"

"W-well, at this point, I should just like to go home," she stammered, twiddling her thumbs nervously.

"*This* scrying mirror will show you things that most mirrors cannot. Simply gaze into its center, little bird."

"That's *silly*. Mirrors can't show you anything other than what they reflect," Bijou replied smartly.

The Giant Moa puffed up his chest and peered over her again. "And little red birds who claim they are, in fact, *not* birds, cannot possibly fall from the sky," he argued.

Bijou rolled her eyes again and crossed her arms over her chest as she sat.

"*This* is my trade, little red bird," the Giant Moa began. "I show the lost what they ought to find."

"But that isn't a *real* trade, or you'd require something in return,"

Bijou insisted. "Besides, if you really want to learn a skill or trade, you must attend school and *become* someone."

The Giant Moa snorted. "What a terribly interesting concept. One is *not* someone until one has *become* someone. I shall alert the artists and poets, builders and bakers, fishermen and mothers. At this news, they shall want to console one another," he recited, glaring down at Bijou, who suddenly felt very sheepish.

"Oh *my*, I did not mean to offend you," she begged. "I suppose I was simply reciting my teachings."

"*Simple*, indeed," he scoffed. "Now, peer into my scrying mirror, little red bird, and visualize where you want to go."

Bijou squinted and looked long into the hand mirror, its black glass beginning to fog and swirl within the golden frame. Suddenly, an image began to materialize in the fog.

"Why, that's my *nursery*!" she exclaimed. "And that's my doll-house! And garden! And Mother and Father sitting by our pond!"

"The mirror knows *all*," the Giant Moa began. "It will take you where you want to go. Wouldn't you like to have it?"

"Well, I *would*," Bijou replied suspiciously, accepting the mirror. "But I have nothing to trade for it."

"How about your lantern? It gets awfully dark in the Wood, you know."

"But it isn't *mine*. I have to return it to the Tree Dweller," Bijou replied. Though she *had* sworn to return the lantern, Bijou had to admit that she was curious as to what the Queendom might be like, and she wasn't sure that she was quite ready to leave the Wood after all. "I'd better get on after the Tree Dweller, or he'll reach the castle before I do."

"Oh *yes*, you really *must* see the tower while you're there!" said the Giant Moa, winking.

"What exactly does the Queen keep in the tower?"

"The tall tower is where the wretch keeps the wishing stars! She locks them away so that no one can wish upon them!"

"But that's *unfair!*" Bijou cried, standing up and stomping her foot into the pile of hay. "No wonder everyone calls her *wretch!*"

"*Do* let us consult the *Oracle!*" the Giant Moa shouted, unfurling his crumpled newspaper. With a swift foot, he reached into his high pants pocket and retrieved a glass monocle attached to a golden chain. Lifting and tucking it before one large round eye, he cleared his throat thoroughly. "See here!" he began. "The *Oracle* reads, my little red bird, that you shall not leave, nor shall you return to the place you wish for most—so says today's *Post*," he recited, lowering his monocle and peering over his paper.

"Nonsense!" Bijou protested. "You made that up!" She wagged her finger at the Giant Moa, who again appeared offended.

He puffed up his chest and cleared his throat once more. "My *dear* little red bird—"

"Will you *cease* calling me 'little red bird'? I've told you—my name is *Bijou*, and I am a girl, nothing more!"

"*Nothing* more, *indeed*," he decided, snatching the mirror back from Bijou and tucking it and his newspaper into his burlap sack. He peered down at her one last time and muttered something insulting beneath his breath before sprinting into the Wood.

"But, *sir!*" Bijou implored, stumbling out of the hay again.

She threw her hands into her dress pockets and kicked angrily at the ground. Climbing the steep pile of hay again, she sat and sulked by the stable and striped stag.

"I won't move another inch in this Wood," she grumbled. "The Queendom will just have to come to *me!*"

# Chapter IX

## The Archer and the Gilded Arrow

The Archer stowed his bow and veiled himself beneath his dark green cloak. He stalked the downed red fowl, stealthily maneuvering through the thick forest. As he approached the pile of hay beside his stable and striped stag, he realized the fowl was not a fowl at all but a girl.

Startled, Bijou sprang to her feet and tumbled clumsily out of the tall pile of hay.

"Dash my *wig*!" bellowed the Archer. "I could have sworn you were a fowl, gal!" He turned a blood-red color and quickly bowed to her on one knee.

"It was *you* who fired an arrow at my wings!" Bijou scolded, wagging her finger at the Archer.

"Come to supper, apple butter!" he pleaded. "I've got rolled roast beast and cheese made up for more than one! There isn't ever more than one, and never more than *me*," he trailed off sadly.

Bijou *was* awfully hungry again, and she felt a bit sorry for the

bumbling man. Her hunger allowed her to forgive him for shooting her out of the sky as well.

*I suppose if I could hardly see him from up so high, then likely, he could scarcely see me from so far below.* She nodded to herself and scooped up her lantern, following behind the Archer timidly.

They hadn't moved but a few feet before the Archer stopped suddenly and sniffed the air about Bijou.

"My *goose* and *gander*! Is that *you*? Great stink of the Phoenix!" he exclaimed. "You *don't* want to leave the stink of the Phoenix's nest on you, foul gal! Do you wish it to track us *both*?"

Without another word from him, and before Bijou could protest, the Archer scooped her into his arms and tossed her over his shoulder. Her scarlet dress flew over her head as he began to run through an overgrown garden toward his cottage. The narrow pathway was lined with giant purple agapanthus flowers, which nearly towered over his small cottage. To Bijou, their petals reminded her of the white dandelions that grew by her pond, and how they looked after one soft blow on their fluffy threads. She grasped at one as they rushed past and heard a faint cry. Its petals turned a pale yellow and fell to pieces in her hand, withering on the spot.

"*P-poor th-thing*," she stammered, waving sadly at the flower while she was being bounced up and down like a rider on a galloping horse.

The Archer threw open the door to his home, then slammed it shut with the same urgency. His home was cozy but modest. A single wooden rocking chair sat beside a large wooden trunk, and a high, sturdy wooden table stood next to a black iron stove, which had something delicious-smelling roasting inside of it. Bijou closed her eyes and sniffed the air as the Archer swung her off his shoulders. He flung his green cloak onto the back of the rocking chair and dusted off his teal tunic and black knee-length riding boots.

"Now, shall we tickle our innards, gal? Tea? One lump or ten?" he offered, grinning a wide and quite menacing grin, then shoving Bijou backward into the seat by the fire.

"But the Phoenix," she began. "I thought you said—"

"Sure, sure, the *tea*," he interrupted. "It'll help shoo that awful *stink*!" The Archer cupped the palm of his hand around his long, pointy nose and waved the other at Bijou.

"I do *not* have an awful *stink*!" she mocked, stomping her foot. She sniffed the air for a moment, realizing that again there *was* quite an odd smell about her, so she accepted the tea, scowling on principle as she sipped it. After a moment had passed, she noticed that the strange stench had gone. Bijou stared down into her teacup, and there was a grimy clump of muck at the bottom.

"*That's* the stink of the Phoenix," said the Archer, grinning satisfyingly and swiping the teacup from Bijou's hand and tossing it into a boiling pot atop the iron stove.

"How did it get in *there*?" Bijou gasped, her mouth dropping wide open. "Did the *tea*—"

"*Ayup*," agreed the Archer quickly, turning on his heels and kneeling by his wooden trunk. He flung open its lid and rummaged about for a moment, tossing various items over his shoulders until finally he produced a miniature gilded arrow. "Gotcha!" he exclaimed, whirling around and placing the arrow in Bijou's hand.

"How shall I use it without a bow?" she asked.

"*Oh*, you don't need a bow to use *that* kind of arrow," he insisted. "Just give a little prick with it."

"What would a little prick do?"

"My dear gal, that depends entirely on *whom* you prick!" he chuckled, offering Bijou a roast beast and cheese roll.

She waved her hand toward the roll, declining, her hunger suddenly fading again and an ill feeling coming over her.

"Great *jar-licker*!" bellowed the Archer. "Only a *savage ingrate* would shoo my *famous* rolled roast beast and cheese!"

"Pardon *me*, but perhaps *your tea* has made me ill!" Bijou spat, grasping at her grumbling stomach.

"My *tea* made *you* ill, did it? Well, if that don't draw the long bow!"

The Archer devoured the roast beast and cheese roll in one bite, then grabbed his cloak from the back of the rocking chair and flung open the cottage door angrily, ushering Bijou out. She protested as he pushed her down the pathway, past the towering agapanthus, and back to the pile of hay near his stable and striped stag.

"But, *sir!* I didn't mean to offend you by not eating your supper. I simply—"

"Nothing further, fowl! Just fly on *home!*" the Archer snapped, throwing up his hand and waving off her response. He leapt onto his rocking stag, gave a kick of his heels on either end of the horse's backside, and it took off into the Wood.

Bijou could hear him grumbling as he went.

"Savage! *Ingrate!*" he called over and over.

"*Well!*" she huffed, never having been rushed so rudely from teatime before.

Along with her illness, Bijou had also begun to feel dizzy staring up the now steep trail of the mossy mountain. She grasped her firefly lantern and swayed nauseously, lecturing herself on the ills of sweet drinks.

"Fowl, you've been put off the drink for good; *stink* or no stink."

# Chapter X

## The Grand Elder Elephant

Bijou didn't feel like herself at all, but she pressed onward, finally climbing to the top of Moon Mountain. The Queendom lay just a short distance ahead, and the outer walls were enormous, made entirely out of stones that had been gold-gilded. It was surrounded by a wide moat that seemed to be filled with a pale sticky pudding in place of water, and Bijou was sure that a castle moat was meant to have some terrible beast living in it to ward off intruders, but *this* moat didn't appear uninviting at all.

"That doesn't seem very secure," she remarked, shaking her head at the sticky pudding.

A gilded drawbridge was pulled to the tall, arched entrance of the outer wall, and Bijou had just begun to walk toward the Queendom when a giant white elephant came stamping out of the Wood behind her.

"*Goodness!*" she cried, tumbling head over feet as the elephant bounded past her.

"*Oh*! What a clumsy, mumsy, nittering thing I am, *oh*!" stammered the elephant in a soft voice. She immediately offered her massive trunk to assist Bijou to her feet.

"*You* should be more careful!" Bijou scolded, wagging her finger at the clumsy elephant.

"I'm terribly sorry, dear, *oh, terribly* sorry!" the elephant bumbled. "Here, let me clean you up," she said, spraying Bijou with hot air from her trunk and knocking her over once more.

"That's quite enough!" Bijou bellowed, leaping to her feet again.

"Are *you* going to the castle too?" the elephant asked, staring down at Bijou curiously.

"I *am*!" she shouted back.

The elephant winced at Bijou's bark, making her feel somewhat sorry for her harsh tone.

"I'm sorry, elephant, but I feel ill from something that I drank, and I have to see the *Queen* soon."

"*I* can take you!" the elephant offered. "You may ride in my howdah!"

"Your *what*-ah?"

"My *howdah*. See?" The elephant pointed upward with her long trunk to the elegant and bejeweled carriage atop her back.

"*Oh*, that would be lovely!" Bijou exclaimed, accepting the step up on the elephant's trunk.

She settled into the comfortable carriage, throwing her feet into the air and onto a pile of silk cushions that had golden tassels fastened to their corners. Bijou threw her hands behind her head and relaxed into her cushioned seat as the elephant stomped toward the moat. "Pardon me, but, *why* are you going to the castle?" Bijou asked, leaning through the open howdah window to better hear the soft-spoken beast.

"The Queen has summoned me all the way from Bombay, you know. *I'm* the Grand Elder Elephant!"

"*Oh*, I have heard of Bombay!" Bijou began. "My father has been there on business many times. But, why have you come to the Queendom?"

"To grow the Queen's sugarbeans, of course."

"What are *sugarbeans*?"

"*What* are sugarbeans?" the elephant gasped. "Sugarbeans are only the most *delectable* bean of Bombay, and they only grow from the tolly briar, which only *I* know how to tend."

"But that's *silly*," Bijou laughed. "I have *seen* tolly briar bushes, and they do *not* grow sugarbeans. Besides, how could an *elephant* tend a garden?"

"Could *you*?" the elephant snapped, giving Bijou a spray of hot air with her trunk.

"*Well*!" Bijou scoffed. "I suppose I could be *taught*!"

"*Quite*," replied the elephant sarcastically.

"Well, what is so *special* about these sugarbeans?" Bijou asked.

"Have you heard of the Kingdom of Bohemia?"

"*Oh*, Father has *met* a Bohemian! Is it in Bombay?" Bijou guessed.

"*Clever girl*! The Maharaja of Bohemia and the Gilded Queen of Moon Mountain are sworn enemies, you know. If I did not carry these seeds from the Maharaja to appease the Queen, there would surely be war once more between them!"

"War over a bunch of *beans*?" Bijou couldn't believe it. "There may as well be a war over a plot of land, or *water*, or *tea*!" she added. Though it was true that her mother and father argued often over seemingly insignificant matters, Bijou simply couldn't imagine a war fought over beans.

"*Anything* the Maharaja of Bohemia has, the Queen of Moon Mountain *demands* to have as well," said the elephant. "Besides, when sliced open just *one* sugarbean instantly transforms into an entire feast! Anything in the Queendom that you could imagine you could have in just one bean!"

Bijou liked the sound of that *very* much and began to wonder if her mother had been growing the wrong kind of tolly briars.

The Grand Elder Elephant stopped at the sticky pudding moat, and a guard who was pacing back and forth on the rampart atop the stone wall began to shout down to her.

"Oi! Have you an invitation?" he bellowed, banging the butt of his spear on the ground.

Though the gentle beast tried with all her might to bellow back, the volume of her voice never rose above soft and serene.

This, Bijou quite appreciated.

"*I* am the Grand Elder Elephant. I bring the tolly briar seeds for the Gilded Queen," she said proudly.

The guard leaned far over the edge of the wall, straining to hear the quiet voice. He gave up quickly and then slumped lazily toward a giant wooden lever. He tugged at the lever, lowering the gilded drawbridge over the sticky pudding moat, and the Grand Elder Elephant stomped over it and under the arched wall into the Queendom. Bijou decided it would be wise to keep quiet inside the howdah, as *she* did not have an invitation.

# Chapter XI

## The Queen's Gilded
## Henchmen Go Mad

The people of the Queendom came out of their homes to see the giant and bejeweled white elephant standing in the center of their market. Bijou peeked out the open window of the howdah and noticed a crew of angry little men wearing gilded suits of armor and gilded helmets to match rushing toward them. To Bijou, they looked like miniature tin soldiers who had been colored gold, and they carried giant nets and long hooked rods twice their own height instead of rifles. Shouting at one another and stumbling, they took great gurgling swills from heavy brown jugs marked *Ale*, and Bijou wondered if that meant they *too* were ill and needed the drink to cure their *ailment*.

*They're mad*, she thought, shaking her head disapprovingly.

"Oi!" shouted one of the men at the elephant.

"You there!" bellowed another little man. "We are the Queen's gilded henchmen, and you've been summoned to court, straight away!"

"*Oh yes*, I *know*," replied the Grand Elder Elephant softly. "I have brought the tolly briar seeds," she added, pulling a silk sack of them from under her tongue with her giant trunk.

The crew of little men raced toward the elephant, their tiny legs barely noticeable under their bulky armor. They began to spread out in a circle, surrounding the elephant, poking and prodding her with their giant hooks.

"Ouch!" she cried, whirling about and shaking the entire market. She smacked one of the giant hooks away with her trunk and pulled another out of a henchman's hand. "You little men ought to mind your manners!" she instructed them as politely as she could.

"What are *they*?" asked a henchman.

Another henchman bonked him over the head with his now empty brown bottle. "Don't be a *buffoon*!" he spat. "Manners are *monsters* that live under our cots and frighten us to sleep!"

"That's not right at all!" Bijou chimed, leaning out of the howdah once more.

"*Who's that*?" shouted a henchman, poking at the side of the carriage with his rod and hook.

"I *said*, that isn't right *at all*!" Bijou repeated, tearing a giant red jewel off the howdah wall and throwing it down at the little man.

It bounced off his helmet, and the henchman became enraged. "*You* don't know a thing about it!" he bellowed back at her. "Manners are *dreadful* little monsters; never could abide them!"

*Clearly*, Bijou thought, rolling her eyes.

"See here, girl, if you haven't an invitation you must go! This elephant has been called to the Queen's court!"

"Well, *I too* have business with the Queen!" Bijou insisted.

"*Not* without an invitation!" the henchmen declared in unison.

One henchman threw down his bottle and the rest of the men did the same.

"To the beast!" one of them bellowed, tossing his net around the front of the Grand Elder Elephant as another henchman threw one around her middle, and another around her end.

To Bijou's surprise, the elephant didn't thrash or blow her trunk. She simply sank into their nets with a somber look on her face.

"Heave-ho! Heave-ho!" shouted the crew in unison, and the Grand Elder Elephant's legs were swept out from under her with a swift and final tug.

Bijou tumbled out of the carriage and through the giant holes of the nets. She scurried to hide behind a nearby butcher's chopping block as the elephant was dragged through the market and toward the castle.

The elephant blinked her bejeweled eyelids and waved her trunk sadly at the cheering crowd.

"*Poor* clumsy thing," Bijou whispered to herself, wanting desperately to free the beast from Bohemia.

# Chapter XII

# The Queen's Gilding Mill and Market

"*You, shoo!*" came a hearty voice from behind Bijou.

She whirled around, startled by the booming voice and stood up to meet the stranger. A giant dressed shabbily in a dusty scarlet jacket and matching red cap stood towering over her with a stern look on his plump face.

"I'm *terribly* sorry, sir, but I was just hiding from those mad little men," Bijou pleaded.

"*Humph,*" the giant grunted, removing his cap, which was two sizes too small for his head, and scratching a sparse patch of hair for a moment. "*You* go castle?" he asked, thumbing toward the towers.

Bijou nodded her head up and down, quickly realizing that the less the seemingly simple giant knew, the better.

"*I* the Miller," he said, lifting back the curtain to his mill and stepping inside with Bijou in tow. He wrapped a dusty black apron around his waist and returned to his tall worktable, selecting a large iron hammer from a pile of tools.

"P-pardon me," Bijou stammered, "but could you help me get into the Queen's court?"

"I work; *you* go," he grumbled back.

"Well, I *have* business with the Queen, but I'm afraid I've misplaced my invitation," she fibbed slightly, shifting her weight uneasily from one foot to the other.

"Then *how* you have business?" he asked, banging his giant hammer down upon a red-hot iron rod he'd taken out of the fire behind him.

"Well, that's difficult to explain," Bijou began, "but, I have a sensible reason, I'm sure." She thought for a moment, but with the Miller's banging, she could hardly hear her own thoughts. "Please, Miller, would you stop banging that hammer?" she pleaded, hopping up and down on tiptoes to see over his tall worktable.

"I work; *you* go castle," he grumbled again, shrugging his shoulders and peering down at Bijou.

"But *how* do I get into court without an invitation?" she persisted.

The Miller sighed heavily, realizing he couldn't ignore Bijou's pestering. He selected a rough iron henchman's helmet from a pile beneath his table, then crudely painted a few thin sheets of gold leaf onto its exterior and placed the helmet in Bijou's hands.

"Wear *court*," he instructed. "*Must* gilded see Queen." Then he quickly shooed Bijou from his worktable and out of his mill. "*I* work; *you* go." The simple but dutiful giant closed the curtain and returned to his work once more.

"My *word*," Bijou whispered to herself, placing the heavy helmet on her head and grasping the handle of her lantern. Her yellow curls poked out from under her helmet in all directions, and she was sure she looked quite ridiculous, but if the disguise was her only way into the Gilded Queen's court, then she too would be gilded.

Bijou passed each shop in the market, sniffing the air and taking in the delectable scents of pies baking and chocolate sweeties being frosted. Peddlers and merchants alike stopped her the entire way down the cobblestone road, enticing her to buy.

"*Aye*! *You*! A sweetie for a sou?" shouted an old woman from behind a market table. Her booth was piled high with bricks of chocolate that were as big as her hand, and she worked quickly to bundle three bricks together before tossing them at Bijou.

"*Oh*, thank you, but I can't buy today, ma'am," she said, removing her helmet.

"It's only a sou, child! 'Aven't ya got a sou?"

"I'm afraid I *don't*, ma'am. I didn't bring my bank."

"'Oo goes to market wi'vout even a sou? It's a small enough amount!" spat the old woman, coming from around her booth to snatch back the bundle of chocolate bricks.

"I'm *sorry*, but I'm merely passing through." Bijou backed away from the persistent merchant and down the cobblestone road a few steps before bumping into another booth and knocking over a barrel of green apples.

"Clumsy clod!" shouted the old woman.

Bijou whirled around and began to scoop up the fallen fruit. "I'm *very* sorry! I didn't see!"

"*That's* because you didn't *look*," came a low voice from inside the shop. An old man appeared from behind a patch-covered curtain and glared in Bijou's direction with a pair of sky-blue foggy eyes. His eyes never fully focused on Bijou's, and she immediately realized that he couldn't see her.

She let the apples fall from her arms into the barrel, and began to back away quietly down the cobblestone road once more. The blind man grasped for his wooden walking stick, slamming it down upon his booth.

"*Where* are we going, clumsy clod?" he huffed.

"I put them all back, sir!" Bijou began nervously, twiddling her thumbs.

"Yes, I did *hear* my apples drop into my barrel, thank *you*."

Bijou blushed, feeling embarrassed. "I *would* buy one if I had a sou," she assured.

"Not even a sou!" taunted the old woman.

"I wasn't intending to buy!" Bijou barked back, stomping her foot.

"Then what are ya doin' goin' to market?" The old woman wagged her wrinkled finger at Bijou, grumbling something unintelligent.

"If I *had* a sou, sir, I'd give it to *you*," Bijou again assured him, while turning to thumb her nose at the nosy woman. "Besides, how much could a few apples cost?"

"More than a *sou*!" the old woman blurted.

The old man remained quiet and calm as he nodded his head in agreement.

"Oh *dear*," Bijou began. "Perhaps I could do some kind of chore for spilling your fruit?"

"*Ha!*" jeered the old woman. "He's just an old fopdoodle! Besides, a clumsy clod can't work for a blind fopdoodle!"

"I *could!*" Bijou insisted, stomping her foot. "Well," she began nervously, "I don't know *how* to work, but surely what I could *learn* would be worth a few spilled apples."

The old man rapped his walking stick on his booth three times. "Do not sell short your worth today, for it will cost twice as much to buy back tomorrow," he said sternly, leaning forward to feel for an apple at the top of the pile. He tossed it in Bijou's direction despite being unable to see, and she caught it.

"But *sir*, I haven't a sou," she insisted.

"*Aye*, she's a *common*, clumsy clod, too! Not even a sou!" taunted the old woman.

The blind man ignored their bickering and slumped back into his shop, closing the curtain behind him.

Bijou placed the helmet on her head and returned to the road. She set the apple down upon a single cobblestone like a hopscotch marker, hopping on one foot and traveling down the road and back again.

"*Common*, clumsy clod!" shouted the old woman. She scowled at Bijou.

Bijou scowled back.

# Chapter XIII

## The Gilded Butterfly and
## the Stone Fairy Bridge

Bijou dusted off the apple and took a bite, stopping before a tall wisteria tree that had grown in the middle of the road. Its flowering branches drooped down to the ground, and its trunk was entirely covered with thousands of blue butterflies, whose brilliant cyan and black wings made the tree appear to move with every minute flutter.

"Such a peculiar place for a tree to grow," Bijou remarked, circling it and admiring the butterflies. She removed her helmet and tossed it to the ground, then leaned in closer to the tree to examine it. She could suddenly see a bit of gold wriggling past the other butterflies, and Bijou bent at the waist to see what it was.

The Gilded Butterfly finally surfaced from under the sea of cyan and lifted off from its section of bark, the wings of the other butterflies shuffling to fill the empty space quickly. It fluttered down the cobblestone road, not stopping as usual to sip from the surrounding purple buddleia butterfly bushes.

Bijou thought they resembled giant scalloped ice cream cones, and she turned one upside down, nestling her green apple inside, and leaned over to give it a lick. "Mmmm," she moaned, imagining an ice-cold sorbet running down her chin. "Green Apple-Mint, Flora Bell's *favorite* flavor!"

The skin of the apple did have a taste, but it wasn't of a delicious Green Apple-Mint as Bijou had pretended. In fact, the more the taste lingered on her tongue, the more it tasted of the Cod Liver Listening Oil that all the mothers on the lane forced their children to endure. The hope was that after each nightly dose they'd listen to and obey their parents more and more willingly, but who *really* knew what was in the stuff.

The Gilded Butterfly began to flutter in and out of Bijou's yellow curls, tickling her neck and calling for her attention, and she swore that she could actually hear the creature talking to her.

"Stop that, *stop* that," she giggled, shooing the butterfly. "*You're* part of the reason I'm in this mess to begin with, you know. What's that? Follow you *where*? I think I'd rather stay on the road, if you don't mind," Bijou replied, scooping up her lantern and continuing down the cobblestone road.

The Gilded Butterfly flew out ahead of her then stopped, hovering on a breeze for a moment where the cobblestone road ended.

"Why has the road ended?" Bijou asked. "Where shall I go *now*?"

The butterfly veered off of the road and beneath a low and narrow canopy of buddleia bushes. It whispered for Bijou to follow, and so she gave a sigh and obeyed.

"Where *are* we going? Isn't the castle the *other* way?" Bijou peppered the creature with questions, but it continued to flutter without pause.

Once it had led Bijou through and to the other side, the Gilded Butterfly turned about immediately, fluttering back beneath the canopy and up the road. It quickly found its place on the wisteria tree and disappeared once more beneath the blue butterflies.

The cobblestone began again where the buddleia canopy ended, and Bijou found herself at the base of a stone bridge that had a sparkling stream flowing beneath its archway. It was made of agate stone, which shimmered in every crevice, and was covered in lush ferns and poppies of every color.

Bijou began to cross the bridge, which seemed to be curiously low at its base and high at its peak for such a small stream. She was sure she could hear the soft sounds of whispers beneath her, and she placed her firefly lantern on the stone ledge, leaning and listening far over the side.

"*Goodness!*" she cried, losing her footing and tumbling over the edge and into the stream below.

"A wet hen *again!*" she bellowed, kicking her feet about in the water angrily.

Bijou fished about in the stream, searching for the gilded helmet and finally discovering it attempting to sink into the stream upside down. She scooped it up angrily and placed it atop her head once more, but the stream water it had collected came gushing out, drenching her again.

"*That's* a funny way for a henchman to behave!" came a tiny voice.

"Who said that?" whispered Bijou, whipping around.

A flowering vine dangled just above a patch of floating lily pads in the stream, and Bijou's eyes followed it upward to a garden growing upside down from the underside of the stone bridge.

"I *said*, that's an awfully funny way for a *henchman* to behave!" the tiny voice scolded again.

Bijou searched about furiously, then suddenly, a flickering violet light flew to her, landing on the top of her nose.

"*Oh!*" Bijou exclaimed, startling the creature.

"*Hush!* Are you trying to wake the entire garden?" it screeched, wagging its small finger at her.

"How could one *wake* a garden?" Bijou demanded. "It's not as if it's alive."

"Says *you*, ninny!" shrieked the voice. "Does a bud not bloom into a flower the same as a child becomes full-grown? And does a vine not change in color as it ages, or become frail when it's ready to die? There are far more plants that cover the land than there are any of *you* or *I*, and they're *all* alive!"

"Well, I'm *sorry* to disturb your garden, but—"

"It doesn't belong to *me*," the creature spat. "I *grew* from it; *all* of the creatures in this garden did."

"You say you *grew* from the *flowers*?" asked Bijou in disbelief.

"Of course!" scoffed the creature. "Where did *you* come from?"

Bijou thought this a curious concept, indeed, and she began to consider whether perhaps *plants* were farming *people*.

"What *are* you?" she asked, poking at the bouncing purple light.

"You shouldn't ask *what* someone is; one is a *who*," replied the creature.

"Well then, *who* are you?"

"Violet Fairy, of course."

"Isn't that a *what*?" asked Bijou.

"It happens to be my *name*. Should I ask a giant like you *what* you are, or should I ask your *name* first?"

"*Oh*, but I'm *not* a giant!" Bijou assured.

"*Precisely.* You're a *who*, and you're a who who woke me from my nap in the poppies, thank *you* very much!"

"I *beg* your pardon, little fairy, but, you see, I fell over the bridge. I did not mean to disturb you."

"Well, *what* is a henchman doing down *here*?" snapped the Violet Fairy. "And since when do they make them so very tall?"

"*Oh*, but I'm *not* a henchman either!" Bijou replied, removing her gilded helmet. "This is my disguise so that I can sneak into the Queen's court."

"*Ha!*" shrieked the fairy. "*Some* disguise! You'll never get through the gates!"

"I fooled *you*," said Bijou, swatting at the creature.

"Well, *hardly*," grumbled the fairy, flying into a crevice in the stone bridge.

"Oh *no*, please don't go," Bijou pleaded. "I don't mean to argue, but I'm soaking wet, and I can't go to court like *this*," she said, standing up and wringing out her hair and dress, and fluffing her ruffled sleeves.

"None of *my* never mind, ninny!" snapped the Violet Fairy, poking its head out of the crevice, then quickly tucking back inside.

"*Well*," Bijou huffed, stomping her foot in the stream, splashing even more water over her clothes. Desperate, she threw herself down on a lily pad and began to sink slowly until she was sitting and pouting in the cold stream once more. She began to weep, placing the helmet back on her head and burying her face in her hands.

The Violet Fairy poked its head out of the crevice again and began to feel sorry for the sopping-wet girl. It sighed heavily and fluttered out of the crevice to rest upon Bijou's wet knees.

"I do *despise* the sound of sobbing," it grumbled. "If you'll stop, I'll help you get dry!"

"Why would *you* help me?" Bijou sobbed.

"Well, if you don't want my help then—"

"No, no, I do, I *do*!"

The Violet Fairy flew once more into the crevice and flew out of it again holding a golden marabou feather that was four times its own length. The fairy began to spin about madly, waving the giant feather over Bijou's hair and dress. Bijou could feel her dress drying faster and faster as the fairy flew.

"I'm completely dry!" she exclaimed, checking her slip and puffing up her ruffled sleeves once more.

"I *told* you I could do it," boasted the creature.

All at once, a mob of the Queen's subjects dressed in their best velvet robes and their necks dripping with gilded jewels, rushed over the bridge and toward the castle.

"Fairy, why do you suppose they're in such a hurry?"

"*Those* are the Queen's subjects, of course. It seems they're late to court again!"

"They're practically falling over one another," Bijou remarked, watching the mob pushing and shoving as they sped toward the castle.

"*All* things appear to move about quickly whilst one is standing still," said the Violet Fairy, placing the golden marabou feather into a giant sunflower, whose petals swallowed it up as they closed. "*However*, the Queen *is* a *wretch*, and she wouldn't hesitate to throw a tardy subject who was even a moment late into the tall tower!" it added.

"*Oh*, the *tower!*" Bijou gasped, realizing she had lost the time. "Well, thank you for your help, little bridge fairy, but I simply must get to the castle, or I'll never get home," she said, grasping her wet lantern and tiptoeing over the stones and back to the top of the bridge.

"*Castle!*" shrieked the Violet Fairy. "I *knew* it; you *are* a henchman!" The fairy began to flutter about Bijou once more, poking and nipping at her.

"But I'm *not!*" Bijou pleaded.

"*Shoo, shoo!*" shouted the Violet Fairy, pulling at Bijou's curls.

"*Oh, fine!*" Bijou growled, stomping over the stone bridge and down the cobblestone road. She picked up her feet even higher to add effect to the stomping. "And I *won't* be back!"

The creature snorted. "Some threat that is!" it shouted after Bijou.

It grumbled sleepily and slid down the tall stem of a sunflower, sinking finally into the closing petals of a purple poppy below. The surly sprite fell asleep inside the flower once more.

The flower fell asleep too.

# Chapter XIV

## The Gilded Queen Calls for Her Sugarbeans

Bijou marched angrily toward the castle gates, suddenly able to hear the steady beat of the Tree Dweller's drum once more. She quickened her pace after it, so determined that she very nearly didn't see an enormous golden hot-air balloon sitting in the courtyard. It had a gilded woven basket and four thick landing ropes tied to four gilded stakes in the ground. Bijou circled the balloon curiously, hopping on tiptoes to peer inside.

"Oi! *You*! You can't be there!" came a pair of angry voices in unison from behind her. A pair of gate guards came rushing toward Bijou with their sharp gilded spears in hand. "That's the Queen's balloon, you know!"

It seemed every place Bijou had been thus far, she had been told what to do and what not to do. "I was merely *looking*," she huffed.

"You're not permitted to *look*!" snapped the first guard.

Each guard clasped one of Bijou's arms and escorted her to the gate. They returned to their posts on either side of the arched entrance to the castle and crossed their gilded spears, preventing Bijou from passing.

"Not so fast!" shouted the second guard. "Have you an invitation?"

"Well, I've been invited, *yes*," Bijou began, fibbing again. "You see, I'm a henchman too," she added, pointing upward to her gilded helmet as the guards began to examine her from helmet to toe.

"The Queen said *nothing* of a *new* henchman," remarked the first guard, scratching his bulbous chin.

"*Oh*, well, I would have arrived sooner, but I fell behind while we were trapping the white elephant," she said, straightening up and saluting the gate guards.

"Well, you'd better get to court!" scolded the second guard, both guards uncrossing their gilded spears in unison. "The Queen will throw you into the tower for being late even a moment!"

"Y-yes, sir—I mean, *sirs*," she stammered, saluting once more, then hurrying through the open gate and into the court.

Bijou crept timidly through the buzzing crowd, which was huddled around a growing scene in the middle of the great hall. As she pushed her way between the Queen's subjects, Bijou could see the Grand Elder Elephant chained by its foot to one of the giant white marble columns that held up the high gilded dome of the hall. All of the brightly colored jewels that once covered the white elephant's head and howdah had been replaced with gold-gilded ones, and she stood solemnly before a tall white marble staircase that led up to a single gilded throne. The back of the throne was nearly as tall as the Grand Elder Elephant, and the seat was piled high with scarlet silk pillows. Behind the throne and draped over every gilded wall were luxurious tapestries and giant gilded phoenix eggs atop gilded stone pedestals. The entire hall was either gilded or white marble, and Bijou could suddenly see spots between each blink from all the shine and glare.

All at once, a crew of pygmy music makers marched from behind Bijou and through the crowd, sounding giant gilded horns and trumpets as they went. The crew marched up the white marble stairs and split off to the left and right of the throne. They stopped playing and lowered their instruments to their sides just as the Queen's henchmen came past, carrying someone inside a grand gilded sedan chair.

"That must be the *Queen!*" Bijou whispered to herself, ducking low behind a row of towering subjects.

The henchmen stopped abruptly in front of the throne, and one of them threw off his rounded armor and fell on all fours beside the opening of the sedan chair. Another held his hand out as a tiny gloved one presented itself from inside. The Queen poked her head out of the sedan chair and scowled at her cowering subjects, who quickly stopped their chatter. Instantly, the entire hall went silent.

Bijou couldn't help but to giggle at the sight of the Queen's hair, which she wore completely gilded, her tightly folded curls piled ten layers high with a gilded and bejeweled crown wavering atop them. She stepped out onto her henchman like a step stool, and he winced as she dug both heeled slippers into his back. Another henchman threw off his armor and fell to the marble floor as well, and the Queen began to walk smugly from one to the other. Her long golden and bejeweled gown blinded them as she walked, and they wobbled uneasily beneath her. The two henchmen switched places over and over, scurrying in front of one another until the Queen reached her throne. One suddenly leapt up to climb atop the other henchman's shoulders, then lifting the Queen upward, he placed her gently on the pile of silk cushions.

"Why, she's only as tall as her gilded hair," Bijou remarked, inching closer to get a better look at the tiny Queen.

"*Who's* the chatternitter chatting in *my* court?" shrieked the Queen, her voice shrill and piercing.

The entire hall stood still for fear that she would call upon them, and her henchmen straightened up, searching the crowd and scowling.

"Whoever spoke, put them in the pudding! That ought to shut them up!" she bellowed.

The crowd began to quake with fear, and someone suddenly started to push Bijou toward the front of the court from behind.

"*Hey*! Stop that!" she shouted, spinning about and coming face to face with the Tree Dweller. "*You*!" she exclaimed, throwing her hands on her hips.

The boy snickered mischievously and beat his drum, then skipped back into the growing crowd, disappearing again.

"*Who's* the nittiwathunger beating that *drum*?" shrieked the Queen, standing up on the pile of silk cushions and peering out into her crowd of subjects.

Bijou had begun to back up slowly when the Queen's gaze suddenly settled upon her.

"*You*!" shouted the Queen, pointing her scepter at Bijou and snapping her fingers. "Nab that nit!"

The mad little henchmen from the marketplace came from behind and, each grabbing a limb, hoisted Bijou into the air and carried her toward the throne.

"Put me down!" she demanded, kicking at the henchmen and squirming free.

The men were still quite mad from their ale drink and began to stumble over one another as they tried to capture Bijou.

"Come to me, henchman!" the Queen beckoned, snapping her tiny fingers.

Bijou shifted her eyes, realizing that she was still wearing the gilded helmet. She gulped and quickly curtsied.

"Remove your helmet!" roared the Queen.

Bijou lifted her bowed head and removed her gilded helmet, her wild yellow mane of curls falling down around her face. The crowd gasped and began to chatter again.

"Silence!" the Queen commanded.

The chatter stopped, and Bijou knew she'd have to think quickly.

"*Majesty!*" she exclaimed, curtsying again. "I have come with the Grand Elder Elephant to deliver your tolly briar seeds!" Fibbing again, Bijou turned over her shoulder to look back at the chained white elephant.

The Queen glared at Bijou, then the white elephant and back again. "*You* brought my sugarbeans?" she shrieked.

"Well, *no*, Majesty," Bijou began. "I brought the Grand Elder Elephant, and *she* brought the tolly briar seeds."

"Then *who* has my sugarbeans?" demanded the Queen, jumping up and down furiously on her pile of cushions.

"Well, you have to *plant* the tolly briar seeds first, Majesty," Bijou replied. "Unless of course," she considered, tapping her chin in thought, "there might be a *wild* field of tolly briars somewhere, Majesty. That *would* be faster."

The crowd let out a wave of snickers, which the Queen quickly silenced with the rapping of her scepter.

The Queen's page, a plump green kakapo parrot dressed in a pair of golden satin knee-length breeches, white satin ruffled blouse, and a golden brocade vest, came from behind Bijou, carrying the silk sack of seeds on a gilded platter toward the throne. The henchmen leapt upon one another's shoulders, creating a tower to deliver the seeds, and the Queen snatched them, spilling them out into her gloved hand.

"*Where* is this *wild* field?" she demanded, tapping a golden slipper impatiently on her cushion.

"I'm afraid I don't know, Majesty. You'd have to find it, I suppose."

"And *how* long might it take for these seeds to grow in *my* garden?"

"Well, I should think a full growing season, Majesty," Bijou said smartly, recalling precisely how long it took her mother to grow a bush.

"Unacceptable!" bellowed the Queen, tossing the golden seeds into the air, her henchmen scattering suddenly to collect them. "I'm famished, and I *want* my sugarbeans *now!*"

"You shouldn't be so greedy!" Bijou scolded, wagging her finger at the Queen.

The crowd gasped and was buzzing with chatter once more, and Bijou looked about uneasily, feeling suddenly as if she'd made a grave mistake.

"What I *meant*, Majesty," she began, smiling and batting her eyelashes sweetly in an attempt to redeem herself, "is that I simply feel sorry for you if you can't appreciate the time it takes for your crops to grow." Bijou couldn't bring herself to coddle the Queen entirely, seeing as she'd been so rude and wretched thus far.

"Only a *fool* feels sorry for a queen! Besides, I have *everything* I want," sneered the Queen.

"And your *subjects?*" Bijou proposed, tapping her foot on the marble floor. "Do *they* have all that they want or need? *You* take their wishing stars from them!"

The crowd gasped again and the Queen turned blood-red.

"Put her in the pudding!" ordered the Queen.

"Preposterous!" Bijou snapped, crossing her arms over her chest. "Do you mean that *useless* moat?"

The Queen ignored Bijou's impudence. "To the sticky pudding moat with her! And make sure she's good and buried in it!"

The mad little henchmen surrounded Bijou again and tossed a net over her head, trapping her beneath it.

"Shoo! *Shoo!*" Bijou barked, kicking at them through the net. "I was simply warning the Queen of how long it would take for the tolly briars to grow!"

"And how would *you* know precisely how long it takes for them to grow?" the Queen snapped, jumping down from her pile of cushions and onto her henchmen's shoulders.

"Well, I don't *precisely*," Bijou began, twiddling her thumbs behind her back and addressing the Queen from beneath the net. "The white elephant knows," she added, motioning toward the chained beast. "I'm sure if you let her go, she will gladly plant the tolly briar seeds, and you shall have your sugarbeans!"

The Grand Elder Elephant nodded eagerly at the Gilded Queen, who merely scowled back at her.

"If that beast from Bohemia tends the briars that grow my beans, then why precisely do I need *you*?" demanded the Queen, grinning smartly from one tiny ear to the other.

"Well, I suppose you *don't*, Majesty."

"Ah-*ha*!" shouted the Queen, rapping her scepter on Bijou's head. "Just as I suspected! Put her in the pudding!"

"*Stop* that!" Bijou yelled, the crowd gasping in unison once more.

"You admit you have no purpose *whatsoever*!" shrieked the Queen, waving Bijou away with her small gloved hand as she ascended to her throne once more.

"Well, I'm *positive* that I can do other things!" Bijou shouted, stomping her foot inside the giant net.

"*Other* things?" sneered the Queen.

"Well," Bijou began, thinking quickly, "I suppose I could tell you a joke!"

"I already *have* a court jester!" The Queen snapped her fingers as a tall, thin man came bumbling toward the throne and began juggling his gilded pins on her command. "See? *Everything* I want!"

"W-well," Bijou stammered, twiddling her thumbs nervously. "*Oh*! I know!" she exclaimed. "What did the chess piece say to the other before bedtime?"

The Queen leaned far over, and while in thought, she tapped her scepter on the jester's floppy hat repeatedly, and he cringed after each rough thump.

"*What* did the chess piece say to the other before bedtime?" the Queen repeated to herself.

"*Knight, knight!*" Bijou exclaimed, chuckling to herself as the crowd of subjects erupted into waves of intense chatter once more.

"Did you *hear* what she said?" asked one subject.

"She said, '*knight, knight!*'" answered another in amazement.

"That's *awfully* clever, isn't it?" remarked a man in one group.

"Yes, *indeed*, that *is* awfully clever!" replied another group in unison.

"*Bravo!*" shouted the crowd of subjects. "How clever is that girl!" they chortled.

Bijou smiled and congratulated herself on her cleverness.

The Queen became enraged and began whirling her scepter about in the air. "Silence!" she bellowed, the crowd going quiet and still again. "You didn't give me enough time to guess!"

"A nit without wit is quick to *outwit*, throws a fit, then quickly quits," recited Bijou beneath her breath. She giggled, and the Queen's mouth began to curl up at one side.

"*What* was that?" growled the Queen.

"Oh, *nothing*, Majesty. Nothing at all!"

The Queen sank into her cushions and pouted, which reminded Bijou of a small child in mid-tantrum. Then, it suddenly struck her why the Queen was so much smaller than her subjects.

*Of course! She's just a small girl!* Bijou thought to herself. *She doesn't know how to rule!*

*She's just a small girl!* thought the Queen, eyeing Bijou while still pouting atop her throne. *She isn't very clever at all!*

Both small girls looked upon one another knowingly now, smiling confident smiles.

"Majesty," Bijou began, thinking quickly, "how long have you been Queen?"

The Queen seemed shocked by the question, and she banged her fist on her lap. "Always!" she insisted.

"But, *Majesty*," Bijou began condescendingly, "there was no one *before* you? Not even your mother or father?"

The Queen opened her mouth wide, but nothing came out. She thought for a moment, then appeared confused.

"*I—*" she began, pausing momentarily, and then lost her thought. "Well, I don't remember." The Queen shifted her eyes about nervously. "I can't remember *when* they made me Queen. The only memory I have of Mother and Father seems like a dream. It was the day the Phoenix clutched me in its talons and dropped me in its nest! Oh, Mother and Father were terrified!"

"Oh *dear!*" Bijou gasped, suddenly feeling sorry for her again. "What did they do, Majesty?"

"Not a thing! They left me high in the baobab tree to fend for myself. But I soon wrangled that Phoenix and rode it all the way back to the castle! That's right!" shrieked the Queen, suddenly recalling the day in its entirety. "I returned from the nest with armloads of giant gilded eggs, and from that day forward, *everything* in the Kingdom had to be gilded like my monster's eggs! *That* day, my father's Kingdom became *my Queendom!*"

"What happened to them, Majesty?" Bijou asked, slightly nervous as to what the answer might be.

"Mother and Father? Yes, I remember now," said the Queen, smirking. "I put the two wretches in the pudding *myself! Now*, to the tall tower with *you!*"

All at once, the mad little henchmen pulled the net from under Bijou, sending her feet into the air above her head. The Gilded Queen took her place inside the grand sedan chair and her court henchmen carried her behind the captured girl as she was hauled through the great hall.

"To the tall tower! To the tall *tower!*" chanted the Queen's subjects as they marched in a line behind her and out of the great hall.

Bijou sank into the net and smiled to herself, once more applauding how clever she'd been. For she had managed her own escort to the tall tower, and there she would soon find the wishing stars.

# Chapter XV

## The Wretch's Pest

*Bom-bom, bom-bom, bom-bom, bom-bom!*

Bijou could see the glow of the drum bouncing between members of the now furious mob as she was carried in the net. The mad little henchmen stopped abruptly, stumbling into one another and letting Bijou loose. A single henchman was quickly volunteered to rap on the tower door, and he tiptoed timidly, scurrying back into the mob afterward.

"Such a fuss!" Bijou grumbled to herself, collecting her lantern and shining it on the giant tower door. It suddenly began to creak and slowly opened.

The mob gasped in unison, backing away as the Queen smirked from her seat inside the gilded sedan chair.

A tall black shadow cast upon the stone tower wall began to descend the staircase, and Bijou gulped nervously and trembled as it came closer.

"It's the B-b-b-black Beast!" stammered the court jester,

dropping his gilded juggling pins and doing a backflip over a row of henchmen.

The mob of subjects became frightened and panicked, and they hurried away from the tall tower as quickly as their long limbs could carry them.

"*Henchmen*, stop them!" commanded the Queen, but her subjects had fled so quickly that now only her court henchmen remained to see the Black Beast. "You there, girl!" she snapped, directing the tip of her scepter toward Bijou. "To the tall tower, you nit! Get on!"

Bijou gulped and held her lantern out in front of her once more as she moved slowly toward the open door. She began to notice that the once massive black shadow was shrinking before her very eyes as it continued to descend the stone staircase. Smaller and smaller it shrank until the black shadow was no bigger than a tolly briar seed.

"*Hulllllooo?*" she whispered through the doorway.

All at once, the shadow began to speed across the stone wall, and a tiny black fly flew through the open door toward her.

Bijou's mouth fell open in shock, and she thought surely there had been some mistake.

"Are *you* the Black Beast?" she scoffed.

"I am, *indeed!*" shrieked the tiny fly, buzzing about Bijou and slicing through her curls.

"Why, you're just a *housefly!*" Bijou exclaimed, breathing a sigh of relief.

"*Just* a *housefly!*" it spat furiously. "*I* am the *Queen's* Black Beast, you know!"

"*Quite!*" chimed the Queen from inside her sedan chair. "To the tall tower with you!" she ordered again, snapping her fingers and commanding that the prisoner be taken.

The tiny fly flew suddenly at Bijou, slicing through her curls again and nipping at her bare arms.

"*Ouch!* Stop that!" Bijou snapped, swatting it away. "*Some* fearsome beast! *You're* not even gilded!" she mocked, flicking at the fly with her thumb and index finger until she had backed it into a corner.

"*Stupid* girl, I'm the *Black* Beast after all! Besides, the Miller *tried* to gild my wings, but it wouldn't stick," added the tiny fly defensively, somewhat embarrassed.

"Well, *I'd* say the wretch *herself* is more fearsome than *you* are! *You're* just the wretch's pest!" Bijou winced and turned to look over her shoulder, realizing that she had forgotten herself again.

The Queen's face was blood-red once more, and Bijou imagined her head turning into a steaming teapot.

"Did you *hear* what she called me?" gasped the Queen. "To the tall tower! To the tall tower!" she bellowed, waving her scepter about madly and giving a whack to each henchman as they juggled her sedan chair atop their shoulders.

Bijou suddenly remembered the Archer's miniature arrow, and she plunged her hand into her dress pocket to retrieve it. She closed

one eye and aimed the gilded arrow at the nearest henchman, throwing it like a dart between the tiny gaps in his gilded armor.

"*Oi!*" he shouted, his entire body shrinking in an instant and disappearing inside his armor.

The Queen's sedan chair began to wobble unsteadily and slid

downward as her henchmen stumbled over one another in an attempt to catch it, but the chair hit the ground nonetheless, and the Queen came tumbling out in a heap. The henchmen gasped in unison and stood trembling and clinging to one another.

"*Who's* the feeble fopdoodle who dropped *my* chair?" roared the Queen's furious voice from beneath her long golden gown.

As the petrified henchmen rushed in a V formation to scoop up the Queen, it reminded Bijou of the wooden pins in a game of Skittles. She removed her gilded helmet, and drawing it backward in her hand, sent it speeding toward the henchmen, bowling them over.

As all their miniature mouths opened to roar and howl, and their miniature bodies flew in all directions, Bijou hurried through the tower doorway, past the tiny housefly, and slammed the heavy wooden door shut behind her. She sped up the stone spiral staircase and to the top of the tower, where before her stood a small gilded door. She knelt down and tugged at the golden knocker, but the door wouldn't open.

"I'm trapped!" she cried, searching about for another way in.

"You *won't* find another door!" shrieked the housefly, zipping up the stone spiral staircase behind Bijou to nip at her.

Bijou flicked at the fly angrily and tried to catch it in her cupped hands.

"*You* tell me how to get into the tower or I'll *squash* you!" she insisted, swatting at the fly as it buzzed about her.

"No one gets in but *me!*" it taunted. "You'll have to catch me if you want through *my* door!"

"*Catch?*" Bijou whispered to herself, suddenly remembering the gilded flute. She reached into her pocket to retrieve the tiny golden instrument, and began to blow softly through its golden mouthpiece.

As a soothing melody whistled through the flute, Bijou could see the fly was beginning to tire and slow in pace. She continued to play,

and the housefly began to fall asleep, finally plummeting through the air toward the floor. Bijou grabbed her lantern and threw it open, catching the tiny fly and trapping it inside.

"Caught!" she cried proudly, setting the lantern on the stone floor.

Bijou had begun to scold the sleeping housefly when a thunderous rumbling suddenly began to sound, and the small gilded door started to stretch and grow before her very eyes.

"*Goodness!*" she gasped, jumping backward and examining the gilded door that was now double her own height.

It creaked and groaned, opening slowly, and Bijou poked her head inside timidly.

"*Hulllllooo?*" she whispered, stepping into the dark room.

A barred window at the top of the tower was the only source of light in the small, round room, and her firefly lantern was of little help in the blackness.

*Bom-bom, bom-bom, bom-bom, bom-bom!*

Bijou whirled around at the sound of the drum, and the boy came skipping through the open tower door.

"*There* you are!" she shouted, stomping her soft buckled slipper on the hard stone floor and lunging toward the boy. "I've got you!" Bijou exclaimed, grasping the Tree Dweller by his drum strap and pulling him to the ground.

As the two fussed at and fought one another, a small light began to flicker and glow in one corner of the room. The pair stopped fighting and lay tangled in a dusty heap, watching as each wishing star woke, one bouncing ball of light at a time.

"*My word!*" Bijou cooed, jumping to her feet and shielding her eyes from the bright glow of the lights. "The wishing stars! I've *found* them!"

"*I* led you to them!" declared the Tree Dweller, placing his hands upon his hips in a proud stance.

Bijou's mouth fell open in shock. "Why, you did *no* such thing!" she grumbled.

"*I* led you with my drum, did I not?" he demanded, wagging his finger at Bijou and pulling at one of her yellow curls. "And besides, *I'm* the marvelous boy who slew the *real* Black Beast, you know. It was a black tiger long ago; it even had black eyes, and the only parts of its entire body that *weren't* black were its sharp gilded claws!" The boy grinned smartly and flicked one of the four glistening gilded claws he had fashioned for jacket buttons. "The Queen replaced the black tiger with a black housefly and never told her subjects that she had!"

"So *that's* why they're so terrified of such a small wretch," Bijou considered. "It's no wonder they all surrender their wishing stars

so freely. Well, *I* shall take care of that! I'll free the wishing stars *myself*!"

"You'll *never* free them without *my* help," said the Tree Dweller, laughing and skipping about madly as the glowing stars bounced in unison, following his lead.

"*Nonsense*," scoffed Bijou, sticking her tongue out at the boy. "I simply have to open the door and let them out, is all. You watch, boy!"

As she began to march toward the gilded door, it swung open suddenly and slammed against the tower wall. The wishing stars trembled, going dark in unison, and the Tree Dweller leapt to the ceiling and cowered as he hung from the barred window. Bijou stood trembling in the center of the room, and she found herself met once more by the furious Gilded Queen and an army of henchmen behind her.

# Chapter XVI

# The Gilded Queen Catches a Thief

"*Thief! Thief!* This nit means to steal *my* stars!" shrieked the Queen, whirling her scepter around in the air and holding up her wavering tower of gilded curls.

"They aren't *yours*, in the first place!" Bijou demanded, stomping her foot. "*You* stole them from your own *subjects!*" she added.

The Queen gasped, snapping her fingers and motioning for her henchmen to lift her up. They tossed her into the air and atop their shoulders, and she stood now at Bijou's height.

"*Everything* in my Queendom is *mine*! And *everything* in the *Wood* is *mine*!" she bellowed, rapping Bijou over the head with her scepter.

"Someone ought to teach you to not be so greedy!" Bijou snapped, wrenching the scepter from the Queen's tiny gloved hand and waving it about at the growing number of henchmen.

"Arrest her! Arrest her! Put her in the pudding!" shouted the Queen furiously.

As a pair of henchmen rushed from under the Queen and toward Bijou, she suddenly remembered the Sweetie Maker's potion. Bijou quickly curtsied before the Queen, bowing low as she offered the scepter upward. The henchmen stopped abruptly, stumbling into one another clumsily.

"*Forgive* me, Majesty!" Bijou exclaimed, fibbing again and winking up at the still cowering Tree Dweller. She smirked and pulled the vial from her dress pocket and held it out to the Queen. "I nearly forgot, Majesty, the Sweetie Maker instructed me to give you this potion."

A henchman snatched the scepter with one hand and the vial with the other, passing them upward to the Queen.

"*Oh*, she *did*, did she?" sneered the Queen. "That portly, plump pumpernickel pie baker hasn't been to court in many moons! This *must* be a delicious sweetie, indeed! Summon the Sweetie Maker, and make it quick!" she roared, whacking a henchman with her scepter.

He rushed to the tower door and called through a small gilded megaphone for the Sweetie Maker, and in no time the portly pie baker, wearing her floppy chef's hat and flour-dusted apron, was escorted into the tower, a henchman on either side of her.

"*Sweetie Maker!*" shrieked the Queen, causing the portly woman to wince and shudder. "Did *you* concoct this potion?"

The Sweetie Maker squinted her eyes and shrugged her lumpy shoulders. "Got me, Majesty," she began nonchalantly. "I make an awful lot of sweeties, you know, and it's difficult to keep track of them *all*, sugar—uh, *Majesty*," she bumbled, her escorts snickering in unison.

"Silence!" shouted the Queen, shooting the escorts a pair of furious glances as they cowered behind the Sweetie Maker. "This *infernal* girl, who has attempted to steal *my* stars, claims *you* sent her to court with it!"

The Sweetie Maker leaned in to get a closer look at the glass vial and studied Bijou for a moment. "*Oh!* You know, Majesty," she began, "I *do* recall concocting that particular potion just *today!*"

"*Well?* What does it *do?*" insisted the Queen impatiently.

Bijou motioned to the Sweetie Maker from behind the Queen and henchmen. She stretched her arm high into the air, wagging her hand far above her head and balancing on tiptoes as she nodded toward the Sweetie Maker.

"*Well*, Majesty," the Sweetie Maker stalled, clearing her throat and studying Bijou once more, suddenly guessing her trick. "Oh yes!" she exclaimed.

Bijou gave a relieved sigh, lowering her hand and coming down off tiptoes.

"It shall make you entirely *grown*, Majesty!" said the Sweetie Maker, curtsying quickly.

"*Grown!*" cooed the Queen. "Sweetie Maker, how marvelous! I suppose we can forgive your long absence from court. I have *always* wanted to be grown, you know!"

"Majesty, why can't you grow larger?" asked Bijou.

"*Older* either, you know," began the Queen. "I cracked a gilded Phoenix egg before it was ready, and I ate it up whole. I haven't grown larger *or* older since that Bad Day."

"What day was that, Majesty?" asked Bijou.

"No, no, it wasn't What Day, it was *Bad* Day," said the Queen.

Bijou furrowed her brow, feeling quite confused. "*When*, Majesty?"

"No, *no*, girl!" bellowed the Queen. "*When* Day comes two days *after* Bad Day, which is one day after *Then* Day, and one day before *Now* Day."

"Well, which day is *today*, Majesty?"

"*Confound it*, girl! It isn't *Which* Day, it's *That* Day!"

Bijou stomped her foot. "*What* day?" she growled.

"*That* Day! *What* Day is tomorrow!"

Bijou could feel her eyes crossing, and her brain felt suddenly put backwards.

"Don't be impudent, girl, or I'll put you in the pudding *myself!*"
The Queen threw down her scepter and wrenched the cork from
the tiny glass vial, devouring the entire drink as greedily as a child
would have. "You portly pie baker, I do believe this is your most
scrumptious sweetie yet!" she added, turning the vial upside down
and tapping every last drop of the delicious potion into her wide-
open mouth.

As the Queen continued to tap the vial empty of its scrumptious
drink, she suddenly felt a rumble from her gilded crown to her
golden slippers, and her body began to shrink even smaller than it
already was. Trembling again, her army of henchmen dropped her
to the stone floor and ran cowering through the doorway, filing
down the spiral staircase and out of the tall tower. The Sweetie

Maker darted out of the tall tower behind them, for she was never entirely sure what her concoctions might do to the drinkers who drink them.

Bijou watched as the Queen grasped her aching stomach and moaned. Little by little she disappeared until she was no bigger than a bridge fairy. Bijou knelt down quickly and pinched the back of the Queen's golden gown between her thumb and index finger, lifting her off the stone floor.

"Serves you right for being so greedy!" she scolded, wiggling the miniature Gilded Queen about in the air.

"Arrest her! Arrest her! Put her in the pudding!" came the Queen's high-pitched voice, but the army of henchmen had gone, and there was no one left to help her.

Bijou removed Madam Mer's music box from her pocket and dropped the furious Queen inside.

"It's no wonder everyone calls you *wretch*!" she spat, smirking as she shut the hinged lid with a *slam*.

The Queen, having no one inside her small box to order about, slumped down into her golden gown and began to pout and kick her tiny legs about wildly. She stopped momentarily and began to wonder who would give the orders at court if not her.

"Who will banish the unruly to the tall tower? How will my subjects be *punished* and put into the pudding when they've been bad? What will become of my *Queendom*? I do hope those wretches appreciate all that their Queen has done for them! They'll *never* get on without *me*!"

Bijou put her ear to the lid of the box and listened, considering the Queen's rantings. After all, it seemed that everyone in the Wood and all in the Queendom served their purposes, and perhaps so did the Queen. She lifted the bejeweled lid of the music box and peeked inside. The Queen stood up immediately, becoming enraged once more.

"Thief! Thief! Arrest her!" she shouted, waving her fists.

Bijou shook her head disappointedly. "Only a *fool* feels sorry for a queen," she said, tisking her twice, then slamming the lid shut for good.

Bijou wound the golden key a few turns, and the Queen stumbled about inside the box, shrieking and calling for her henchmen as she did. The soothing plings and plongs began to play, and the furious Queen suddenly felt less furious. She no longer had the energy to protest, and sank again into her long golden gown, falling fast asleep in a heap.

Bijou slipped the music box into her dress pocket and called up to the cowering boy.

The Tree Dweller leapt down from the barred window and beat

wildly on his glowing drum. "Not bad!" he exclaimed. "For a dull *girl*," he added coyly, tugging gently at one of Bijou's yellow curls.

"But boy, who shall rule the Queendom now?"

"*Oh*, there will be another, I'm sure," he replied. "There has *always* been a Queen of Moon Mountain, you know." He winked at Bijou and began to beat his drum low but steadily.

The hidden wishing stars came alive at the sound, glowing brilliantly once more. The balls of light began to bounce and dance in the air as if hypnotized by the drum, and they formed a line behind the Tree Dweller as he bounded off the walls and out the tower door, leading them.

Bijou scooped up the firefly lantern and raced after the Tree Dweller. "But boy, your lantern! I took it from your banyan tree, and I knew it wasn't mine, but I was going to return it, I promise!" She held it out to the boy, but he waved it off quickly.

"It isn't *mine either*," he replied nonchalantly. "*I* stole it from a gypsy, who probably stole it from a pygmy. And *he* probably stole it from a—well, you understand."

Bijou frowned, slightly sour that she'd given up trading it for the Giant Moa's scrying mirror. She placed the lantern in the center of the tower room and waved goodbye to the fireflies. As she shut the tower door behind her, she slid the miniature flute into the keyhole and a soft breeze began to blow from outside the barred window and through the instrument. It sounded a single note continuously, and the wretch's pest stayed fast asleep.

The Tree Dweller continued toward the spiral staircase, the bouncing wishing stars in tow. Bijou raced after the boy, following the bouncing balls of light down the spiral staircase and out of the tall tower.

The Tree Dweller beat out a quick and deliberate pattern, and all but one wishing star flew suddenly into the Queendom, and some into the Wood, in search of the wishers they belonged to.

"*Oh*! This one must be *my* wishing star!" Bijou cooed, kneeling before the single remaining glowing light. She closed her eyes and made her wish quickly, and the hovering ball of light began to fade, and finally disappeared.

Suddenly, a roaring noise came from the courtyard, and Bijou opened her eyes and leapt to her feet. She ran through the castle gates and out into the courtyard, where she found the Queen's hot-air balloon awaiting her. The Tree Dweller quickly threw off the four thick landing ropes and leapt into the gilded basket. He pulled on the levers above him, and the giant golden balloon began to lift off the ground. Bijou hopped into the basket at the last second, and the pair floated over the courtyard as the Queen's mob stumbled over one another to watch.

The pygmy music makers sounded their trumpets and horns from the iron gates of the castle, and the mad little henchmen rushed into the courtyard, tossing their gilded spears into the air furiously toward the balloon.

The Giant Moa stood on one gangly leg and held his glass monocle to his eye as he stared up at Bijou in awe. "How *unordinary!*" Bijou could hear him exclaim from down below.

The Archer appeared suddenly, and raised his giant golden bow, sending a fury of gilded arrows flying through the air and toward the balloon, each merely bouncing off the gilded basket like fireworks exploding in the air.

"Down, fowl, *down!*" he bellowed angrily, sending another fury of arrows into the sky.

Bijou tossed the gilded music box over the edge of the basket toward Madam Loulou de la Mer, who was dancing about idiotically. "Catch the wretch!" she shouted down to her.

The gypsy caught the box in her bejeweled hands, but dared not even crack the lid to peek inside, and instead began to dance idiotically toward her gilded caravan, tossing the music box inside and climbing in after it. The pair of sad-eyed warrah wolves took off down the cobblestone road and through the market, towing the caravan behind them as they fled out of the Queendom and into the Wood once more.

"Pardon *me!*" scoffed the Great Auk Potter, tipping his bowler hat to the Sweetie Maker, who had collided with him while chasing a band of henchmen in circles.

"*You* have *not* been invited!" she shrieked, holding one henchman upside down and shaking a half dozen stolen jelly rolls from under his gilded armor, while she whacked at another with her rolling pin.

The Grand Elder Elephant came stomping out of the castle just then, and through the Queendom, bounding into the Wood and dragging behind her the golden chain still attached to her leg.

"Boy, *look*, the beast from Bohemia is *free!*" Bijou exclaimed, jumping up and down in the balloon basket as the Tree Dweller dangled upside down by the back of his knees from the levers.

As the Queendom began to shrink in the distance, Bijou sank into the gilded basket, resting against a thick pile of coiled landing ropes.

*How marvelous!* she thought, shutting her eyes and imagining how surprised everyone at home would be to see that she'd arrived there in a *royal* hot-air balloon.

# Chapter XVII

## Return to the Daydream Door

Bijou rubbed her tired eyes and sat up to peer over the edge of the balloon.

"Boy, isn't that your banyan below?" she called up to him over the roar of the burners. She uncoiled and heaved one of the heavy landing ropes up and over the rim of the basket as it began to hover steadily over the tree.

"I don't need a rope, *dull* girl," the Tree Dweller mocked, giving her a nudge with his elbow and motioning upward to the balloon's giant golden parachute.

"But how will you get down otherwise? Don't you want to go home?"

"I don't need to get *down*, dummy; I need to get *up!*" The Tree Dweller tugged at the dozens of levers and pull-strings above him, causing the fire to roar from the burners once more.

"But *where* are you going?" Bijou insisted.

"*Up* to my daydream door!"

"*Daydream door!*" she exclaimed. "Aren't you afraid that you won't return if you go through it?"

"*Who* told you such a *fool* thing?"

"Madam Loulou de la Mer did!"

"That old *troll?*" the Tree Dweller spat. "She's mad! Mad old Mer! Besides, I come and go through my door *all* the time! I leave it in the night's sky, just past the gilded moon. See it?"

He pointed, but Bijou saw nothing except the setting sun.

"The *night's sky?*" she scoffed, unconvinced.

The boy conked Bijou over the head with a lever he'd pulled from the workings. "You *wouldn't* leave a door in the *day's* sky; you'd burn up, dummy."

"But *how* could someone leave a *door* in the sky?" she demanded, stomping her foot.

"I couldn't very well leave it in the Wood where just *anyone* could find it. Golly, don't girls *ever* stop talking?" he mocked, returning to his work.

Bijou blushed, embarrassed again.

The Tree Dweller ripped another lever from the workings and tossed it at Bijou's head, and she ducking, growling at him.

"*Why* are you ripping out all those levers?" she demanded. "You'll break our balloon!"

"*Precisely!*"

"But you *can't!* I wished to go home, and my parents are bound to be so worried by now!"

The Tree Dweller groaned. "What *are* these parents you keep on about?"

"They're not a *what*," Bijou insisted, "they're a *who!* Or, is that *whos?* Well, they're *lovely*, boy, and I'm sure they're positively *sick* over my whereabouts!"

"These parents, they will miss you if you don't return?" he asked, growing interested in the concept.

"Terribly!"

"They will *forget* you if you don't return?" he kept on.

"Of course not!"

"They will *replace* you?"

"Never!"

"*Ah*," sighed the boy longingly, "that *does* sound all right, I suppose. Perhaps *I* could have these parents? Could we share them? Would I carry them about inside my pocket, or perhaps my drum? Are they really quite small? I think I could manage. It *is* awfully lonely at times to be so alone," he trailed off.

"I thought you said you knew *every* friend and foe in the Wood?" Bijou asked, tapping her foot.

"I *do* know them all," he began, "but, they don't really know *me*. They forget me quickly because they must. I could not do my job otherwise."

Just as Bijou had begun to feel sorry for the boy, she realized he had already lost the thought entirely, and his momentary sorrow had been replaced by his enthusiastic destruction of their balloon.

"Boy, I'm *going* to use *this* balloon to get home!" she asserted.

"Suit *yourself!*" the Tree Dweller warned, yanking at one last lever. The boy grasped the edges of the parachute as it detached suddenly from the gilded basket. He grinned slyly, waving to Bijou as his parachute began to float softly on the wind, and as Bijou's basket began to plummet downward.

A tiny creature, no bigger than a firefly, came buzzing suddenly from above the golden parachute. It wore a green grass skirt and had gilded marabou feathers for hair that swayed about in the breeze. Its wings were transparent and veiny like a fly's, and it spoke not a word as it flew to the Tree Dweller, landing gently on the tip of his nose and fluttering its wings as it balanced on tiptoes. There came another tree spirit suddenly from above the parachute, and another from below, until the boy was entirely surrounded by the creatures. They each pulled at a section of parachute and began to flutter their wings even faster. The Tree Dweller slipped inside of the golden

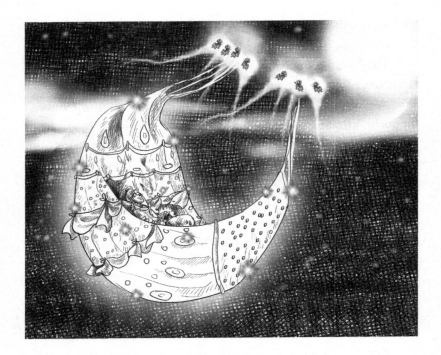

parachute like a giant hammock, and it rose quickly as he was carried higher into the sky and toward his daydream door.

The boy rubbed his unusually tired eyes, attempting to blink out the blur, when a pair of shadowy figures appeared before his gilded door in the sky. They seemed to wave him on, and he wondered how anyone could have found his door after he'd so cleverly hidden it.

"I'll dash them!" he growled, snarling at the shadowy figures. "I'll dash them to pieces, if I must!"

The Tree Dweller's memory had never been long, and his attention seldom held for longer than it took for someone or something to acquire it. But then it struck the boy that he had daydreamed at sundown, even if only for a moment, and of *parents*, at that. The shadowy figures before his door did indeed seem small enough to put in his pocket, and, after all, the marvelous boy would only keep them for as long as he could remember to, or until it was time for *them* to forget the marvelous boy.

* * *

The gilded basket plummeted downward toward the ancient banyan below.

"*Gooooooooooodneeeeeeeeeess!*" Bijou cried, grasping the rim tightly as the woven basket began to unwind from the center outward.

She yanked desperately at one of the coiled landing ropes, but realized that there was something weighing it down. She gave a final heave to the heavy rope, and a shiny gilded anchor attached at its end came flying up and over the rim. The anchor flipped in the air and came down upon a strong limb of the banyan like a grappling hook, its sharp ends digging into the bark of the tree. The unraveling basket continued its rapid descent, crashing through smaller branches and passing the strong limb as the slack of the landing rope began to tighten.

As Bijou braced for impact, the landing rope jerked the basket upward for a moment. She gripped the rim with all her strength as she soared beyond the limb and into the air before she began to fall quickly past the limb again like a yo-yo. The shred of basket that remained now dangled from the landing rope just above the mossy ground.

Bijou peeked from behind the rim and inspected the ground beneath her. The basket swayed above the line between mossy ground and the small blue pond that had first led her to the Tree Dweller's ancient banyan. Since the pond didn't lead to a moving body of water, she knew that meant there was likely but one way out of the Wood—and that was the way she came.

Bijou took a deep breath and jumped from the dangling basket and into the blue water below. She sank quickly like before, the light peeking through the surface of the water fading fast as she disappeared into the lower muck. The water and muck began to swirl

about Bijou in a familiar way, and she was spun into a whirlpool again and hurtled through the other end into darker water.

She kicked frantically toward the surface and burst through, desperate for a breath and sucking in all the fresh air she could while rubbing the water and muck from her eyes. She treaded water momentarily, then used her arms to paddle toward land. Bijou hadn't realized it until then, but after spending the day in this pond and that pond, and despite her terrible fear, she had taught herself to swim.

The drenched girl climbed out of the water and onto the mossy grass. As she wrung out her dress, Bijou's eyes followed a giant and familiar structure before her from its stone foundation to its golden top, and she realized she stood once more before the gilded arched door of the windmill.

# Chapter XVIII

## The Trapdoor in the Floor

Bijou hurried to the gilded door, yanking on its giant golden knocker, but again the stubborn door wouldn't budge.

"I'm *right* back where I started again, and I *still* can't get inside!" she grumbled, kicking the moss beneath her soft buckled slipper and collapsing into a sobbing heap. "I'll *never* get home! I'll be stuck in this Wood forever!" Bijou buried her head in her hands, thinking of her poor pets, and how they were sure to be worrisome and lonely without her.

The golden sun had set, and the vast sugarcane fields and surrounding Wood were even darker and more ominous now. Bijou looked up from her tear-filled palms, sniffling and snorting as she wiped her face with the ends of her white ruffled slip. She had sat and sobbed long enough to dry off, and the gilded moon's glow suddenly illuminated an object that was swaying above her head, catching her eye.

"*That's* the same tangled vine as before," she said, standing up and reaching on tiptoes toward it. The vine now dangled from the windmill's open upper window, and Bijou began to scale the tower's stone foundation. "*Gotcha!*" She grasped the vine tightly with both hands and wrapped her legs around it as she began to pull herself upward.

Finally reaching the open upper window, Bijou peered inside timidly, wondering if anyone was home, or if it *was* anyone's home at all.

"*Hullllooo?*" she called, her nervous voice echoing through the dark interior and back again. She decided, given her uncomfortable position clinging to a vine, that it was not only safe, but the *only* way inside, and so she gave a final yank and burst through the open window.

She had expected there to be a second level of the windmill, but instead Bijou found herself plummeting again.

"*Gooooooooodneeeeeeeeess!*" she bellowed, falling through the air and onto the hard stone floor far below.

Bijou looked about, studying the dark and dusty room, and felt quite as if she were back inside the tall tower of the castle. "Nobody lives here *at all*," she remarked disappointedly, realizing there were no living quarters.

There stood merely a set of large wooden gears rotating before her, and there were no sounds save for the gears and their grumblings.

"*These* must be connected to the windmill blades," Bijou decided, examining them from afar for a moment. "I *wonder*," she trailed off, thinking back on what the Tree Dweller had said about the wind. "If the wind directs or *is* directed in *one* direction, then perhaps if I turned these gears the *other* direction, the wind would *change!*"

Though this notion would have seemed quite impossible any other day, Bijou had already witnessed *nearly* impossible and some *quite* impossible events all day thus far, so she thought it worth a try.

Bijou approached the lower gear and gave a steadfast push on its wooden shaft in the opposite direction until a loud rumble sounded, and the room started to shake. The wheels refused to turn any farther, and a strong wind began to blow through the open upper window, carrying a swirling dust cloud through the entire round room. Bijou coughed and waved her hands frantically at the gray dust as she spun about, and as it began to settle, she found herself standing directly before an open trapdoor in the floor.

"That *must* be the way home!" Bijou cried, hurrying through the trap and down a gilded staircase beneath its opening.

Once at the bottom, she came upon another gilded staircase, only this one went up instead of down. Bijou looked about inside the dark hole. There was nothing inside of it but the connecting gilded staircases and a glimmer of light peeking through a corner section of ceiling. She could suddenly hear her mother calling her to supper, and wasting no time, she tore up the second staircase toward the glimmer of light and burst open a second trapdoor.

Flora Bell poked his head inside the dark hole just then, giving a curious meow, and Bijou knew that she was home.

*Mowe, mowe!* meowed Flora Bell, pawing downward at Bijou desperately.

Bijou leapt from the staircase and into her nursery, scooping up her cat and kissing him all over.

"Flora Bell, did you *ever* think you'd see me again, darling?" she cried, squeezing him tightly as he gasped for breath and meowed in protest. Bijou placed him gently on her bed and gave a tap to his head. "Now, you sit right there, darling; I've got *so* much to tell you!"

Flora Bell simply purred and pawed back at Bijou, and having no concept of time, he hadn't a clue how long his girl had been gone; he only knew that she had been and that he was glad she was back.

The yellow-and-white parakeet began to sing excitedly, and Bijou flew to his round birdcage, throwing open the small door and holding her finger out for him to hop upon.

"Chirps, you *sweet 'keet*! Have you been keeping Flora Bell in line?" she asked with a smirk, pretending to be stern. "You wouldn't believe all the curious birds I met today! *Oh*, and I have *quite* a few bird *jokes* to tell as well!" Bijou gave a pat to the white tuft of feathers on his head and placed him back inside the cage, leaving the door open.

This freedom, the bird appreciated very much.

Bijou picked up her music box from the dresser and brushed her fingers over the gilded engraving of a butterfly on its hinged lid. The familiar plings and plongs began to play as she wound the golden key, and she scooped up her favorite white wooden elephant figurine that sat atop the fireplace mantel. She kissed each of the sapphire jewels that had been reglued many times to the top of its head, most having fallen off from wear over the years. It was still her most favorite present her father had ever returned home with. Bijou ran her finger across its engraved label, which read "Bombay Trading

Co."—and "For my curious & darling daughter, Bijou, a bejeweled keepsake for my jewel," which her father had added himself.

A glimmer of light began to shine through the open nursery window, and Bijou flew to the ledge and peered out at the navy-blue night sky. She searched for her favorite star—the one she always spoke to—and the golden moon suddenly illuminated it as it always did.

"*There* you are," she cooed, winking at her star as it twinkled back. "*Where* have you been? Well, I suppose I know, don't I? I'll have to keep an eye on the Queendom, won't I? I *don't* want to hear that you've been captured again! And that *wretch*! I'll have to tell you *all* about—" Bijou stopped short, then gasped, suddenly remembering her paper dolls.

She hurried to her dollhouse, closing the gilded trapdoor and sliding the two ends of the Tudor-style home back together. She poked at the blue front door with her finger, checking again to see if anyone was home, and there in the elegant foyer were the miniature mossy footprints of the Papier family, and a pile of worn luggage beside them.

"I *suspect* they've been on the trail through the Wood," she remarked to her pets, smirking and closing the tiny door.

Bijou's mother called her sternly to supper once more, and she leapt up, dusting off her scarlet dress and primping her ruffled sleeves. She was both amazed and impressed with herself that she had been on so many adventures that day, yet had managed not to tear a single thread of her clothes. Even her stern mother would have to be proud.

"Coming! I'm *coming!*" Bijou called, sniffing the air and following the delectable scent of her mother's sticky pudding through the nursery door.

Because Bijou could hardly wait to tell her mother and father where she'd been, she hadn't noticed the trail of green moss her soft buckled slippers had left through the hall as she went. Flora Bell trailed after her and thought at first that the moss was likely from their own yard. But then again, he often tracked in mud and moss from their yard and knew it well, and this moss was unfamiliar in a way which none but a curious cat would ever notice.

Bijou's excitement was unwavering that evening, and though her parents seemed impressed with what they thought was their daughter's blossoming imagination, she was positive that she'd actually been to all the curious places she'd seen that day.

"*Oh*, but Mother, I *did* fall from a baobab tree! I saw the Giant Moa with my *own* eyes, and he hypnotized me for a moment with his scrying mirror! Then, the Archer—who was a *madman*, if you ask me—fixed a tea that simply *sucked* the stink—I mean, *stench* of the Phoenix's nest out of me as if it were a magical tea!"

Bijou's mother nodded, humoring her daughter as best she could, but she wasn't really listening, focusing instead on the batter in her mixing bowl that she was whipping with her strong arm.

"Father, I *did* see the Gilded Queen, you know. And do you know that she was younger than I? *I* might have left her stranded in a baobab tree *myself*! In fact, if *I* were that dreadful a wretch, I wouldn't blame you for leaving me in one either!"

But Bijou's father had important business, and was busy shuffling through old maps and papers, and so she retold the stories over and over to herself and her pets that night.

Many moons had passed and the drum still hadn't sounded from beneath Bijou's floor a second time, and she had begun to wonder if it *had* all been a daydream. Still, this uncertainty did not deter her from listening intently for the drum each time she passed through her nursery or played with the Papiers of Number Nine Nursery Row. She knew it would come again. She *knew*, because she *believed* it would.

And then one day, it did.

*Bom-bom, bom-bom, bom-bom, bom-bom!* came the drum.

*Mowe, mowe!* meowed the curious cat.

*Chirp, chirp!* called the 'keet.

Then, down, down crept the curious child once more through the trapdoor in the floor.

\*   \*   \*

*All* instinctively curious children discover the Wood. They must go down to get up and through to get back, but they all find their way eventually. The way may lay beneath a bed, behind a bookcase, kept in a closet, or just down from a dollhouse, but rest assured it *is* there to be found by all those who believe it can be. For, you see, imagination is often fleeting as we grow, and come one day the door will *surely* close.

The End

Begin Again

CPSIA information can be obtained
at www.ICGtesting.com
Printed in the USA
BVOW03*0629171217
503002BV00004B/8/P